英語認證測驗
國際標準版

New TOEIC 新多益

全真測驗

速戰速決400題

作者 入江泉 / 審訂 宮野智靖

命題趨勢全掌握，得分訣竅快易懂

貝塔｜語測
檢測學習平台

iRT+題測 高點｜美語系列

CONTENTS

第一回　全真測驗

第二回　全真測驗

第一回
全真測驗

Model Test 1

＊ 聽力部分的錄音內容從 MP3 001 開始。

＊ 答案卡置於本書末，請自行撕下使用。

LISTENING TEST

The Listening test allows you to demonstrate your ability to understand spoken English. The Listening test has four parts, and you will hear directions for each of them. The entire Listening test is approximately forty-five minutes long. Write only on your answer sheet, not the test book.

PART 1

Directions: For each question in PART 1, you will hear four statements about a picture. Choose the statement that best describes what you see in the picture and mark your answer on the answer sheet. The statements will be spoken only once, and do not appear in the test book.

Statement (C), "They are wearing glasses," is the best description of the picture, so you should mark (C) on your answer sheet.

1.

2.

GO ON TO THE NEXT PAGE ➡

3.

4.

5.

6.

GO ON TO THE NEXT PAGE

PART 2

Directions: In PART 2, you will hear either a statement or a question and three responses. They will be spoken only once, and do not appear in your test book. Choose the best response to the question or statement and mark the corresponding letter (A), (B), or (C) on your answer sheet.

7.   Mark your answer on your answer sheet.

8.   Mark your answer on your answer sheet.

9.   Mark your answer on your answer sheet.

10. Mark your answer on your answer sheet.

11. Mark your answer on your answer sheet.

12. Mark your answer on your answer sheet.

13. Mark your answer on your answer sheet.

14. Mark your answer on your answer sheet.

15. Mark your answer on your answer sheet.

16. Mark your answer on your answer sheet.

17. Mark your answer on your answer sheet.

18. Mark your answer on your answer sheet.

19. Mark your answer on your answer sheet.

20. Mark your answer on your answer sheet.

21. Mark your answer on your answer sheet.

22. Mark your answer on your answer sheet.

23. Mark your answer on your answer sheet.

24. Mark your answer on your answer sheet.

25. Mark your answer on your answer sheet.

26. Mark your answer on your answer sheet.

27. Mark your answer on your answer sheet.

28. Mark your answer on your answer sheet.

29. Mark your answer on your answer sheet.

30. Mark your answer on your answer sheet.

31. Mark your answer on your answer sheet.

PART 3

Directions: In PART 3, you will hear several short conversations between two or more people. After each conversation, you will be asked to answer three questions about what you heard. Choose the best response to each question, and mark the corresponding letter (A), (B), (C), or (D) on your answer sheet. The conversations do not appear in the test book, and they will be spoken only one time.

32. What is the woman's problem?

   (A) Her document is missing.
   (B) Her computer is not functioning.
   (C) An e-mail address is incorrect.
   (D) A file is not complete.

33. When should the files be sent?

   (A) By 2:00 P.M.
   (B) By 3:00 P.M.
   (C) By 4:00 P.M.
   (D) By 5:00 P.M.

34. What does the man suggest the woman do?

   (A) Call the design engineer
   (B) Revise the file
   (C) Log onto a different computer
   (D) Use a delivery service

35. What does the woman ask the man to do?

   (A) Send her a refund
   (B) Give her a new purse
   (C) Repair her purse
   (D) Offer her a discount

36. What does the woman like about her purse?

   (A) Its design
   (B) Its size
   (C) Its price
   (D) Its texture

37. What will the man probably do next?

   (A) Make a telephone call
   (B) Choose a different purse
   (C) Visit another branch
   (D) Pay by check

38. Why is the woman calling?

   (A) To ask for her account balance
   (B) To make a payment
   (C) To renew a contract
   (D) To apply for a card

39. What condition does the man mention?

   (A) The minimum balance for an account
   (B) Credit scores to open an account
   (C) Qualifications to be new members
   (D) The time limit of the interest rate

40. What does the woman ask the man to do?

   (A) Review a charge
   (B) Send her a document
   (C) Increase her credit limit
   (D) Confirm receipt of her e-mail

41. Who most likely is the man?

   (A) A customer
   (B) A technician
   (C) A salesperson
   (D) A receptionist

42. What does the man want to talk to Ms. Shen about?

   (A) Late documents
   (B) Office equipment
   (C) Computer repairs
   (D) Brochure design

43. What is Ms. Shen's plan for today?

   (A) Meeting customers
   (B) Dealing with shareholders
   (C) Reorganizing schedules
   (D) Talking with staff

GO ON TO THE NEXT PAGE ➡

44. What is the purpose of the man's call?

(A) To submit a progress report
(B) To confirm a delivery time
(C) To revise technical information
(D) To prepare a presentation

45. Where Is Mr. Adjani now?

(A) At a building site
(B) At his desk
(C) In his apartment
(D) In a meeting

46. What will the woman do next?

(A) Start a meeting
(B) Phone Mr. Adjani
(C) Get contact information
(D) Read a text message

---

47. Where most likely is the man?

(A) In a printer factory
(B) In a product warehouse
(C) In an engineering office
(D) In a customer service center

48. What does the woman prefer about TZ inkjet cartridges?

(A) Availability
(B) Functionality
(C) Quality
(D) Familiarity

49. What does the woman decide to do?

(A) Track a delivery online
(B) Look at a different Web site
(C) Accept the man's suggestion
(D) Sell the office supplies

---

50. Where most likely are the speakers?

(A) At an airport
(B) At a hotel
(C) At a travel agency
(D) At a restaurant

51. What problem does the woman mention?

(A) Attitude of staff
(B) High prices
(C) Long waiting lines
(D) Lack of room service

52. What does the man recommend the woman do?

(A) Settle her bill online
(B) Line up early
(C) Change rooms
(D) Wait a few minutes

---

53. What are the speakers discussing?

(A) A recruiting program
(B) An upcoming event
(C) Employee benefits
(D) Office schedules

54. What does the woman mean when she says, "You've got to be kidding"?

(A) She is surprised by what the man said.
(B) She disagrees with the man's opinion.
(C) She sympathizes with Margaret's situation.
(D) She appreciates the man's humor.

55. What is mentioned about Ms. Kang?

(A) She commonly assisted colleagues.
(B) She frequently went to Chicago.
(C) She usually provided funding for projects.
(D) She often helped at parties.

---

56. What does the woman ask the man to do?

(A) Inform Mr. Howell of her schedule
(B) Give Mr. Howell her phone number
(C) Confirm her schedule
(D) Get hold of some documents

57. What does the woman mean when she says, "by all means"?

(A) She needs to buy a new file for the trip.
(B) She cannot be contacted if there is an emergency.
(C) She will be able to receive telephone calls.
(D) She has to think carefully before making a decision.

58. When does the woman prefer to be contacted?

(A) At noon
(B) In the afternoon
(C) At any time
(D) In the evening

---

59. What are the speakers talking about?

(A) Upcoming promotions
(B) Hiring strategies
(C) Overseas expansion
(D) Regional markets

60. What is a stated goal of Marcel and Vicki?

(A) Getting local experience
(B) Recruiting more staff
(C) Enrolling in a university
(D) Learning a language

61. How is the man using his lunch hours nowadays?

(A) To prepare for a trip
(B) To improve his skills
(C) To contact universities
(D) To do research on South America

Coupon

Axton Foods Co.

Wake up Feeling Fresh!

Take **$5 Off** coffee, any brand in store

Valid through October 31.

62. Why is the man looking for a certain product?

(A) He wants to try healthy foods.
(B) He read about it in a publication.
(C) He has tried it out before a few times.
(D) He needs to rate it for his blog.

63. Look at the graphic. How much will the man pay?

(A) 5 dollars
(B) 10 dollars
(C) 15 dollars
(D) 20 dollars

64. What does the woman encourage the man to do?

(A) Purchase an additional bag
(B) Go to a Web site
(C) Fill out a membership card
(D) Apply for a new account

GO ON TO THE NEXT PAGE

Floor	Tenants
5	Bilo Investments Jowon Media, Inc.
4	Wannable Textiles Deni Biomedical
3	Aril Publishing Somtlo Engineering
2	Cimin Lighting, Inc. Rea Catering
1	Gillo Realty, Inc. Ashik Software Co.

65. Why did the woman come to the building?

(A) To visit an apartment
(B) To retrieve a lost item
(C) To go to an interview
(D) To rent an office

66. Look at the graphic. What floor does the woman have to go to?

(A) Floor 2
(B) Floor 3
(C) Floor 4
(D) Floor 5

67. What does the man recommend the woman do?

(A) Take an elevator
(B) Change a nameplate
(C) Check the information displays again
(D) Update her online profile

68. What is the woman asking about?

(A) How to obtain an ID
(B) How to pay a bill
(C) How to get to a branch office
(D) How to apply for a job

69. Look at the graphic. What area does the woman work in?

(A) Operations
(B) IT
(C) Administration
(D) Research

70. According to the man, what should the woman do after she gets an employee card?

(A) Take another photo
(B) Deactivate her old card
(C) Carry it with her at all times
(D) Report to the marketing department

PART 4

Directions: In PART 4, you will hear several short talks. After each talk, you will be asked to answer three questions about what you heard. Choose the best response to each question, and mark the corresponding letter (A), (B), (C), or (D) on your answer sheet. The questions and responses are printed in the test book. The talks do not appear in the test book, and they will be spoken only one time.

71. What is the speaker calling about?

(A) A job interview
(B) An interview result
(C) A schedule change
(D) A job description

72. What did the speaker do a few days ago?

(A) Talked with Michael on the phone
(B) Left a message about an interview
(C) Sent a letter with an application
(D) Transferred to the personnel department

73. How long does Michael have to respond?

(A) One day
(B) Two days
(C) Three days
(D) Four days

74. What has delayed the aircraft?

(A) Planes ahead of it
(B) Obstacles on the runway
(C) Mechanical safety check
(D) Bad weather

75. How much longer will the plane have to wait?

(A) 10 minutes
(B) 20 minutes
(C) 40 minutes
(D) 45 minutes

76. What are passengers traveling to Mexico City advised to do?

(A) Follow previously stated information
(B) Get a travel update at their destination
(C) Board from a different gate
(D) Contact airline staff upon disembarkation

77. What is the report mainly about?

(A) Luxury markets
(B) Corporate performance
(C) Economic trends
(D) Business investments

78. How much do analysts expect profits to rise for the year?

(A) 4 percent
(B) 6 percent
(C) 12 percent
(D) 16 percent

79. What does the report imply?

(A) Shopping trends are changing.
(B) CEO policies are failing.
(C) More customers are coming into stores.
(D) Online sales are decreasing.

80. What is the speaker doing?

(A) Introducing a product
(B) Cleaning a house
(C) Helping a customer
(D) Arranging a program

81. What does the man imply when he says, "it'll be spotless in seconds"?

(A) The cloth will dry fast.
(B) The surface will be clean quickly.
(C) The chemicals need time to mix.
(D) The cleaner cannot remove all dirt.

82. What are some listeners invited to do?

(A) Ask the speaker questions
(B) Participate in a demonstration
(C) Talk about their experiences
(D) Receive product samples

GO ON TO THE NEXT PAGE

83. What is the main purpose of the talk?

(A) To develop a curriculum
(B) To explain the existing service
(C) To ask for donations
(D) To inform parents about a new facility

84. What is a feature of the center?

(A) Child computers
(B) Protective enclosures
(C) Special teachers
(D) Expanded curriculums

85. What will Aaron Cummings talk about?

(A) The history of the center
(B) Future plans
(C) The details of activities
(D) Ways to sign up

86. Who is the talk most likely intended for?

(A) Corporate shareholders
(B) Financial reporters
(C) Company employees
(D) Market researchers

87. What success is mentioned by the speaker?

(A) A reduction in production costs
(B) An increase in stock prices
(C) An increase in revenue
(D) A reduction in working hours

88. What does the speaker mean when she says, "I believe you should get credit"?

(A) She considers sales to be adequate.
(B) She hopes higher goals will be achieved.
(C) She owes money to her staff.
(D) She thinks her employees deserve a reward.

89. Which department does Richard Slater normally work in?

(A) Accounting
(B) IT
(C) Consumer Finance
(D) Planning

90. What does the man mean when he says, "I know this is an added burden for us"?

(A) He wants to have more staff.
(B) There will be another position available.
(C) A department will be divided into two.
(D) The company will face some hardship.

91. What will the listeners do next?

(A) Offer opinions
(B) View a presentation
(C) Ask questions
(D) Write monthly reports

92. Who most likely is the speaker?

(A) A business expert
(B) A company president
(C) A news reporter
(D) A communication specialist

93. According to the speaker, what does the report say is necessary for a good presentation?

(A) Practice while in university
(B) Substantial mastery of material
(C) Thorough relaxation exercises
(D) Advanced speaking techniques

94. What is preparation particularly effective for?

(A) Making points clear
(B) Choosing a topic
(C) Facing the public
(D) Replying to inquiries

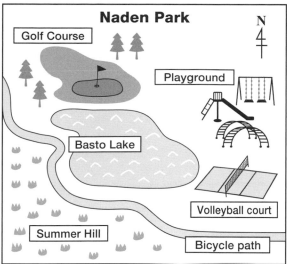

Naden Park

Golf Course

Playground

Basto Lake

Volleyball court

Summer Hill

Bicycle path

N

KASIK PAINT CO.

Office Supplies Order Form

Order Number: 903H2

Item	Units ordered
Desk lamps	8
Photocopier ink	6
Laptops	4
Fax machine	1

95. What type of event is being prepared?

(A) A talent contest
(B) A marathon
(C) An outdoor gathering
(D) A local tour

96. Look at the graphic. Where will the company staff meet?

(A) At the golf course
(B) At the volleyball court
(C) At the playground
(D) At Summer Hill

97. What has already been sent companywide?

(A) Travel coupons
(B) Public transportation passes
(C) Directions to the venue
(D) A list of festivities organizers

98. Look at the graphic. How many laptops does the company need in total?

(A) 3
(B) 5
(C) 6
(D) 7

99. According to the telephone message, what has the company recently done?

(A) Improved its headquarters
(B) Processed a claim
(C) Hired some staff
(D) Changed a launch date

100. What is the listener asked to do?

(A) Train recruits
(B) Adjust a price
(C) Make a phone call
(D) Wait for a text

This is the end of the Listening test. Turn to Part 5 in your test book.

GO ON TO THE NEXT PAGE

101. Mr. Krishna informed the company of ------- plan to visit several important clients on the West Coast the following week.

(A) its
(B) it
(C) he
(D) his

102. Genetic advances at Warsaw Pharmaceuticals mean it may soon be possible to protect people from a ------- variety of diseases.

(A) long
(B) wide
(C) thick
(D) high

103. Director Rao convinced the board to begin export sales to Europe this year, ------- at least lay the groundwork for doing so.

(A) while
(B) since
(C) but
(D) or

104. Alistair Properties Co. ------- to closing most deals in dollars, but due to client demand began accepting euros and yen as well.

(A) accustomed
(B) had been accustomed
(C) will accustom
(D) will have been accustomed

105. First Harbor Pharmaceutical Inc. is one of the top private caregivers in the province and ------- is a leader in advanced medical research.

(A) since
(B) whichever
(C) although
(D) moreover

106. CEO Brian Greene stated at the meeting that an increase in sales of 13% by the end of the year was quite -------.

(A) attains
(B) attaining
(C) attainable
(D) attainably

107. Sun Lady bath soap is certainly ------- than any similar product in fine stores today.

(A) fragrant
(B) more fragrant
(C) most fragrant
(D) fragrance

108. Mr. Ephron wished there ------- more funds for the company picnic, but the employees seemed satisfied with the snacks and beverages provided.

(A) is
(B) are
(C) would
(D) were

109. News reports indicate that some corporations are preparing ------- an economic upturn by making large investments now.

(A) for
(B) and
(C) to
(D) but

110. Ms. Singh made it her personal ------- to track the company's profit margins in each of the major regions it operated in.

(A) interesting
(B) interest
(C) interestingly
(D) interested

111. Evertrue Media Corporation is ------- the number one firm in the entertainment industry in terms of market share.

(A) responsively
(B) undoubtedly
(C) mutually
(D) compassionately

112. Greater Vancouver, particularly during times of economic slowdowns, is ------- many Canadian IT companies locate their offices.

(A) how
(B) why
(C) when
(D) where

113. Mr. Anwar's design team was ------- on time with all its projects, causing the company to rely on it a great deal.

(A) invariable
(B) invariant
(C) invariably
(D) invariability

114. Trainor Inc. maintains a competitive bonus system ------- order to motivate staff in all of its departments.

(A) in
(B) by
(C) from
(D) at

115. Five cents of every dollar ------- on goods in the Tyler Department Store goes toward local charities that help children.

(A) credited
(B) cashed
(C) paid
(D) spent

116. Mr. M'Krumah is in ------- of the company's Lagos branch, operating all its major business activities in West Africa.

(A) responsibility
(B) touch
(C) charge
(D) engaged

117. ------- a sensation among teenagers, the Jumping Box online game rapidly became popular throughout East Asia.

(A) Creates
(B) Creating
(C) Created
(D) Create

118. Director Kim is an ------- fine scholar in the field of robotics, as well as being a good businessman.

(A) intrusively
(B) oppositely
(C) exceptionally
(D) affordably

119. Real estate prices in Hanoi are expected to rise by as much as 15% ------- the local business boom continues.

(A) and
(B) but
(C) as
(D) or

120. Mr. Armatelli feels that ------- is certainly the best way to resolve any problems among co-workers.

(A) talking
(B) has talked
(C) talks
(D) will talk

GO ON TO THE NEXT PAGE

121. Mr. Larson used to work for the Imperial Builders, but he found a new job with Central Constructions three years -------.

(A) else
(B) soon
(C) ago
(D) already

122. The marketing department came up with an excellent plan, but relied on local salespeople for proper ------- of it.

(A) execute
(B) execution
(C) executed
(D) executively

123. Passengers must show the boarding passes ------- were given to them in the ticketing area prior to boarding the aircraft.

(A) what
(B) whose
(C) that
(D) who

124. Umagi Corporation's new steel ------- its shape and strength even when exposed to very high temperatures or pressures.

(A) sustenance
(B) sustains
(C) sustainably
(D) sustainable

125. This MP3 player is guaranteed against breakdowns caused by the manufacturer's ------- during shipping.

(A) warranty
(B) mindset
(C) default
(D) negligence

126. Mr. Nagy always brought a keen ------- perspective to trends in global manufacturing.

(A) analysis
(B) analyze
(C) analytic
(D) analytically

127. After successfully producing 20,000 units last year, the Rabo Corporation's Brazil subsidiary was able ------- on its own as a manufacturer.

(A) had stood
(B) to stand
(C) standing
(D) stood

128. Connor Furniture Inc. has been selling top brands for over 21 ------- years in major cities across the country.

(A) straight
(B) direct
(C) connected
(D) totaled

129. Passengers ------- internationally must go to Terminal D, which houses all gates for overseas flights.

(A) travel
(B) to travel
(C) traveling
(D) traveled

130. Packages that ------- from Los Angeles may take up to five days to arrive in Cairo using Interprize Express Service.

(A) original
(B) originate
(C) originally
(D) originating

PART 6

Directions: There is a word, phrase, or sentence is missing from parts of each of the following texts. Below each text, there are four answer choices for each question: (A), (B), (C), and (D). Choose the answer that best completes the text and mark the corresponding letter on your answer sheet.

Questions 131-134 refer to the following letter.

January 14
Marie-Therese Deneuve
34 Rue de la Croce
Marseilles

Dear Ms. Deneuve,

We are pleased to present you with a business loan of up to €250,000. We are offering this

------- because you are one of our most valued customers with an excellent credit history.
131.

-------. You only have to pay an interest rate of 6.7%. This is a rate you are unlikely to find
132.
------- else. This special rate is available ------- to a selected group of valuable customers such as
133.   **134.**
yourself. If you would like to discuss this offer further, please call me at 008-7745-3009 ext. 19.

Sincerely,

Xavier Bayer
Senior Customer Service Representative
Bank of West Marseilles
The Bank to France, the Bank to Europe, the Bank to the World

131. (A) requirement
     (B) inquiry
     (C) request
     (D) opportunity

132. (A) Your loan application is incomplete as it
         is.
     (B) We would also like to inform you of
         another positive aspect.
     (C) We cannot help you any further at this
         point.
     (D) Interest rates are not favorable in
         today's economy.

133. (A) somewhere
     (B) anywhere
     (C) everywhere
     (D) nowhere

134. (A) according
     (B) close
     (C) thanks
     (D) only

GO ON TO THE NEXT PAGE

Questions 135-138 refer to the following e-mail.

To: Michael Chen <michael.chen@goldcrestbanking.ca>
From: Orianne Durand <orianne.Durand@tzdesign.com>
Subject: Update
Date: Wednesday, February 23

Dear Mr. Chen,

We ------- the revised visuals for the design of your company's new gym shoe, *Street Tiger*.
    135.
Please see the PDF files attached ------- the composition of the materials and the internal structure.
                                   136.
Our apologies for the extra time necessary to complete the revisions.

Our art directors are still ------- your suggestions from last week's meeting into the logo you want as
                            137.
well. -------.
     138.

Thanks again for choosing us to create this very important new product for you.

Sincerely,

Orianne Durand
Chief Designer
TZ Design Ltd.

---

135. (A) will complete
(B) would have completed
(C) have completed
(D) have been completing

136. (A) show
(B) shows
(C) shown
(D) showing

137. (A) integrating
(B) articulating
(C) evaluating
(D) asserting

138. (A) Please make sure to keep it in a safe place.
(B) We hope to show you the selections during Monday's presentation.
(C) You might already have noticed some necessary changes.
(D) Apart from that, they were considered acceptable.

Questions 139-142 refer to the following article.

According to the latest research, more and more employees are suffering from stress in the workplace. -------. In one study, 43% of employees ------- as being under heavy stress had
    139.   **140.**
weak concentration and poor work performance. Corporations operating in highly competitive environments commonly prefer to extend current employee work hours ------- hire new staff, but
                      141.
such long hours invariably lower employee productivity.

Women combining motherhood with careers were found to be at particular risk; -------, reports
                        142.
from workplaces imply that working mothers may experience exhaustion from the responsibility of balancing both homes and jobs. Experts recommend corporations expand the number of daycare centers to reduce their burdens.

139. (A) Reports suggest it is a serious problem among all levels of workers.
(B) It has become of great importance to a successful job search.
(C) Both men and women have been found to be unaffected by such difficulties.
(D) Research shows that many employees are confused by this concept.

140. (A) are described
(B) will describe
(C) described
(D) to describe

141. (A) more than
(B) less than
(C) than not
(D) rather than

142. (A) specific
(B) specifically
(C) specify
(D) specification

GO ON TO THE NEXT PAGE

Questions 143-146 refer to the following notice.

Travel and Weather Update
EuroLine Bus Corporation

*************** Update for the Eastern European Region **************

Bus service on the Prague to Sofia route is currently experiencing severe delays due to sudden and heavy rainstorms. The ------- flooding has affected many places. Roads in such areas have become
          143.
impassable because of these high waters, ------- have closed them to vehicle travel of any kind.
              144.

Travelers are advised to check the main terminal board for the latest information on arrival and departure times. Passengers preparing ------- on any buses at the gates are advised to wait. Buses
            145.
there will leave only when the weather clears enough for them to do so.

-------.
146.

---

143. (A) innocuous
(B) anticipated
(C) interrupted
(D) consequent

144. (A) what
(B) that
(C) which
(D) those

145. (A) departing
(B) will depart
(C) to depart
(D) departed

146. (A) Finally, the scheduled departure times have now been posted.
(B) Please continue to watch this board for further updates.
(C) Thank you to all who have participated in our bus tour.
(D) We hope you will continue to enjoy the weather during your trip.

PART 7

Directions: PART 7 consists of a number of texts such as e-mails, advertisements, and newspaper articles. After each text or set of texts there are several questions. Choose the best answer to each question and mark the corresponding letter (A), (B), (C), and (D) on your answer sheet.

Questions 147-148 refer to the following table.

Travel information for The Irish Princess				
Destinations (from Cork)	**Gibraltar**	**Tenerife**	**Antigua**	**Aruba**
Estimated arrival date	17th	20th	22nd	24th
Present Travel Status	Arrival on Schedule	Updating	Updating	Two days late
Medical Certificate required	No	Yes	No	No
Visa Requirements	Not required for EU residents	Necessary for stays over 30 days	See Passenger Service for Updates	Not required for EU residents

IRELAND-CARIBBEAN CRUISE LINES INC.

147. On what date will passengers on The Irish Princess most likely arrive in Aruba?

(A) 20th
(B) 22nd
(C) 24th
(D) 26th

148. Which destination requires a visa for stays over a month?

(A) Gibraltar
(B) Tenerife
(C) Antigua
(D) Aruba

GO ON TO THE NEXT PAGE

Questions 149-150 refer to the following text message chain.

Sam Porter   9:00 A.M.
Our clients from Gron Paint Co. called to say that their plane has just touched down. They won't be here for another hour, but I'll have Tim meet them at the front door.

Chang Ying Li   9:02 A.M.
Okay. I'm getting out of the subway now. I'll be in the office in about 15 minutes. Make sure that we have paint samples set up for them to review.

Sam Porter   9:04 A.M.
I've laid out 30 of our most popular colors on a demonstration table.

Chang Ying Li   9:06 A.M.
I should have guessed. You always have a handle on things. Good job.

Sam Porter   9:07 A.M.
Also, the conference room is already arranged, with plenty of coffee and tea.

149. At 9:06 A.M., what does Chang Ying Li mean when she writes, "I should have guessed"?

(A) Mr. Porter often anticipates needs.
(B) Mr. Porter must make a decision.
(C) Mr. Porter requires further advice.
(D) Mr. Porter usually follows instructions.

150. What does Mr. Porter indicate that he will do?

(A) Call some clients
(B) Have someone meet a group
(C) Wait by a door
(D) Get some samples tested

Questions 151-152 refer to the following memo.

MEMORANDUM

To: All Staff
From: Sven Bjorg
Time: 10:45 A.M., Wednesday
RE: Christian Jonson

Dear Staff,

As you already know, Christian is leaving us this Friday after more than 30 years with the firm. Before taking his present job as head of Research, he worked in various areas, including Production—both here and in Oslo—Design, and IT. Over the last 18 months, he has been overseeing the highly successful Z45-t drug trials in Zurich.

He has been an invaluable member of Lind Technologies and I know he will be sorely missed by his colleagues and friends. However, I am happy to say he has agreed to stay with us for the next four weeks in a part-time capacity so we will benefit from his expertise.

I hope you will join me and the rest of the Board of Directors for a Bread and Cheese Reception in the Premier Boardroom this Friday afternoon from 4:30 P.M. to formally congratulate Christian on his retirement and wish him every success in his new life!

Thank you,

Sven Bjorg
Managing Director
Lind Technologies

151. Which department is Mr. Jonson working in now?

(A) Research
(B) Production
(C) Design
(D) IT

152. What will Mr. Jonson do over the coming month?

(A) Contribute personal knowledge
(B) Conduct a job search
(C) Hire part-time workers
(D) Attend a board meeting

GO ON TO THE NEXT PAGE

Installation Guide for your Sparkle White Dishwasher
Wonder Electronics Co.

Install the appliance in accordance with the instructions below.

- **Ensure that the appliance is not connected to any power outlets during installation.**

- **Do not remove any of the metal plates covering electronic components or wiring inside.**

- **Confirm the power supply of the residence is compatible with this appliance. If it is not, a converter will be necessary (sold separately).**

- **Install this appliance on a flat surface. Failure to do so could severely affect its stability.**

- **Connect the appliance's water tubes to the main pipes beneath your sink. Check the diagram on the back of the appliance for the correct procedure.**

- **Following installation, please dispose of the packaging in an environmentally friendly way.**

For more information on this and other fine appliances made by Wonder Electronics Co., go to www.wonderelectronicsonthenet.com.

153. What is NOT listed as an installation step for the appliance?

(A) Checking that the electrical supply is suitable
(B) Contacting company technicians
(C) Ensuring positioning is on a surface that is level
(D) Referring to graphs on the device

154. What are users suggested to do?

(A) Test the appliance when installation is complete
(B) Replace the water pipes beneath the sink if necessary
(C) Disconnect the power supply when not in use
(D) Consider the environment when discarding items

Questions 155-157 refer to the following e-mail.

| * E-mail * | ✕ |

From:	Thiago de Silva <tdesilva@ozatmail.net>
To:	Lucia Morais <lucia.morais@olivehotel.fr> Manager, Olive Hotel
Date:	Wednesday, October 7
Subject:	My room

Dear Ms. Morais,

Two weeks ago I e-mailed you to reserve accommodations, along with an online deposit to secure them. — [1] —. I was scheduled to check in tomorrow, so that I can attend the European Manufacturing Conference there in Lyons.

However, I have recently been accepted into a 1-week international management development course in Switzerland, so I would like to cancel my reservation. — [2] —. One of the original team members has had to drop out for health reasons and I have been offered his spot. — [3] —. I realize this is extremely short notice, but considering these circumstances I am hoping I can still get my money back.

Please e-mail as soon as possible to let me know. — [4] —. I hope to hear from you before then.

Kind regards,
Thiago de Silva

---

155. What is the purpose of the e-mail?

(A) To schedule an arrival
(B) To confirm a transaction
(C) To state a change
(D) To make a payment

156. What is a stated concern of Mr. de Silva?

(A) Room availability
(B) Hotel amenities
(C) Refund policy
(D) Cancellation deadlines

157. In which of the positions marked [1], [2], [3] and [4] does the following sentence best belong?

"I have to leave for the training program within the next 12 hours."

(A) [1]
(B) [2]
(C) [3]
(D) [4]

GO ON TO THE NEXT PAGE

Questions 158-160 refer to the following instructions.

How to use Eazee Breeze in your washing machine

Measure out Eazee Breeze Detergent concentrate (1 scoop per medium load of clothes) into a cup of lukewarm water and allow it to dissolve completely for about 5-10 minutes or until it can no longer be seen. Turn on your washing machine, choosing the shortest cycle and making sure your soiled clothes are fully immersed in water. Next, pour the Eazee Breeze mixture onto the clothes. Let clothes soak for at least 15 minutes to allow Eazee Breeze's fast-penetrating formula to work on grime, stains and odors.* Next, close the lid and continue the cycle. With Eazee Breeze you can say goodbye to scrubbing, cut down on wash time and save on electricity.

* Eazee Breeze is safe for all types of fabrics, but as a precaution do not soak dark clothes and whites together.

158. What is the first step in using Eazee Breeze?

(A) Letting the substance melt
(B) Soaking clothes in water
(C) Letting water sit for 15 minutes
(D) Washing clothes for 5 minutes

159. The word "soiled" in line 5 is closest in meaning to

(A) rough
(B) shabby
(C) dirty
(D) old

160. What are people using Eazee Breeze advised NOT to do?

(A) Add extra concentrate
(B) Scrub items before washing
(C) Use together with other products
(D) Combine colors and whites

Questions 161-164 refer to the following online chat discussion.

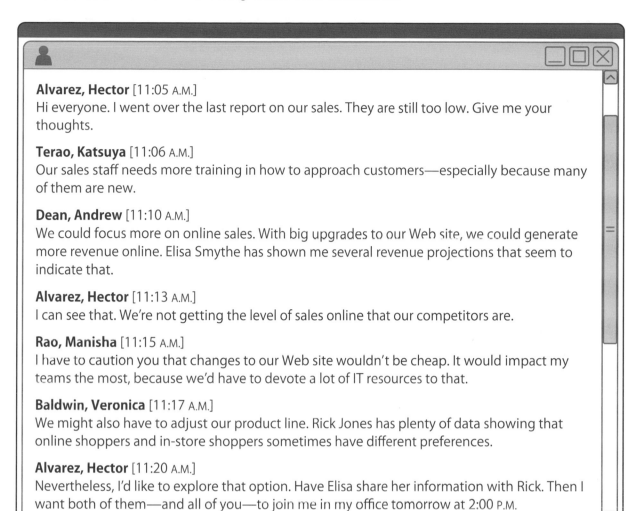

Alvarez, Hector [11:05 A.M.]
Hi everyone. I went over the last report on our sales. They are still too low. Give me your thoughts.

Terao, Katsuya [11:06 A.M.]
Our sales staff needs more training in how to approach customers—especially because many of them are new.

Dean, Andrew [11:10 A.M.]
We could focus more on online sales. With big upgrades to our Web site, we could generate more revenue online. Elisa Smythe has shown me several revenue projections that seem to indicate that.

Alvarez, Hector [11:13 A.M.]
I can see that. We're not getting the level of sales online that our competitors are.

Rao, Manisha [11:15 A.M.]
I have to caution you that changes to our Web site wouldn't be cheap. It would impact my teams the most, because we'd have to devote a lot of IT resources to that.

Baldwin, Veronica [11:17 A.M.]
We might also have to adjust our product line. Rick Jones has plenty of data showing that online shoppers and in-store shoppers sometimes have different preferences.

Alvarez, Hector [11:20 A.M.]
Nevertheless, I'd like to explore that option. Have Elisa share her information with Rick. Then I want both of them—and all of you—to join me in my office tomorrow at 2:00 P.M.

161. At 11:05 A.M., what does Mr. Alvarez mean when he writes, "Give me your thoughts"?

(A) He has to meet a deadline.
(B) He needs to update an account.
(C) He hopes to persuade a supervisor.
(D) He wants to gather some opinions.

162. For what type of company do these people most likely work?

(A) A retail outlet
(B) A consulting agency
(C) A cyber security firm
(D) An event planning company

163. According to the discussion, whose department would be most affected by Mr. Dean's suggestion?

(A) Mr. Terao's department
(B) Ms. Rao's department
(C) Ms. Baldwin's department
(D) Mr. Jones' department

164. What information will Ms. Smythe most likely share with Mr. Jones?

(A) Training methods
(B) Customer profiles
(C) Financial statistics
(D) Team organization

GO ON TO THE NEXT PAGE ▶

Shanghai Romance

MUSICAL LOVERS WILL LOVE THIS NEW PRODUCTION FROM THE RED BALLOON PERFORMANCE COMPANY.

◆

Chosen Best Musical by the Evening Star Monthly!

Set in China in the 1920s, this lavish extravaganza will thrill and excite you!

Read what people are saying about it:

> **"I'm not much of a theatergoer, but I loved it!"**
> –Amy Winters, university student, Edinburgh

> **"If you want lighthearted entertainment for the whole family, this show is for you. We and the kids had a grand time seeing it."**
> –Frank Coswell, business owner, London

Don't miss out on Helen McTavish's performance as Eleanor Gantry. Also starring Richard Mace as Ewan Lockhart.

Tickets are available at the box office from May 18, with online sales starting the day before. Reserve yours anytime until June 20. Seats can otherwise be obtained at the door. The final performance will be on June 27 unless extended.

Discounted matinee performances are held at 2:00 P.M. every Saturday and Wednesday for £35-£40. These cannot be purchased online or used in combination with group discounts or season passes.
For more details, call the Box Office (9:30 A.M. – 11:00 P.M., Monday through Saturday), at 0845-671-1200 or visit us online at www.thamestheater.co.uk.

* Refunds available up to half an hour before each performance begins, less fees.

165. What is indicated about Shanghai Romance?

    (A) It has an international cast.
    (B) It is a show for adults.
    (C) It is a long running show.
    (D) It has received favorable reviews.

166. Who has praised Shanghai Romance?

    (A) The theater owner
    (B) Audience members
    (C) Play writers
    (D) Stage actors

167. When can the earliest tickets be purchased?

    (A) May 17
    (B) May 18
    (C) June 20
    (D) June 27

168. How can guests get lower prices?

    (A) By attending afternoon performances
    (B) By purchasing tickets online
    (C) By seeing the performance twice
    (D) By contacting the performers

GO ON TO THE NEXT PAGE ➡

Questions 169-171 refer to the following e-mail.

* E-mail *	✕
From:	Joseph Mooresville <joseph@gentryparts.au> President & CEO Gentry Car Parts Inc.
To:	Emiko Takeda <emiko.takeda@ichigoauto.co.jp> Purchasing Director Ichigo Automobile Corporation
Date:	September 4
Subject:	Your visit

Dear Ms. Takeda,

Here are the directions you requested. They should bring you directly to our main factory outside Melbourne.

As you drive out of the airport, get onto Highway Nine going west. Take that for about 15 kilometers, until you reach the Pettigrew Overpass. Continue on for an additional 3 kilometers to Exit 3. Take that exit and it will lead you to Coldicote Road. Turn right there, and head north for about 4 more kilometers.

After you pass the Herald Hotel on your right, you'll only be a minute or two away from us. If you see Blake Stadium, you'll know you've gone too far, so make a U-turn at Carlton Park or East Pacific Bank and come back toward us.

Guest parking inside the facility is free, but please be sure to enter one of the spaces marked for visitors. My assistants, Marsha Jensen and William Marsden, will meet you at the gate and see you through security. You'll be able to see them as soon as you pull up.

If you have any questions at any time, please e-mail me at the address above. Or you are welcome to contact me by phone. I look forward to seeing you soon.

Sincerely,

Joseph Mooresville

World Specialists in Car Parts Design

169. How far is Ms. Takeda instructed to drive down Highway Nine?

(A) Three kilometers
(B) Four kilometers
(C) Fifteen kilometers
(D) Eighteen kilometers

170. What landmark will Ms. Takeda see before she reaches the Melbourne factory?

(A) Herald Hotel
(B) Blake Stadium
(C) Carlton Park
(D) East Pacific Bank

171. What should Ms. Takeda do upon arriving?

(A) Park outside the facility
(B) Show her guest pass
(C) Contact security
(D) Look for Mr. Mooresville's staff

Big Changes at Diaz Motors

Diaz Motors yesterday announced substantial changes at the company's assembly plants in Guadalajara, where it employs 3,200 people, and Veracruz, where it employs 1,200. From April 1, staff will work four-day weeks and take 20% reductions in base salaries. — [1] —. This policy will be subject to a 12-month review, at which time it will be decided whether to continue it.

CEO Felipe Kahlo said the move was designed to secure the long-term competitiveness of the company. — [2] —. Earlier this month, Diaz introduced a voluntary layoff program and eliminated 300 part-time jobs at its subsidiary component plant just outside of Mexico City. Diaz's board of directors has also reportedly discussed outsourcing some processes to lower-cost Guatemala.

— [3] —. According to the latest statistics, car purchases from Diaz and other South American automakers have fallen by 63% over the past three months. This decline is despite a $US 200 million investment the company made recently in advanced production technologies. Diaz stock held steady in light trading on the announcement.

Union officials are reported to be in negotiations with company representatives over ways to avoid further layoffs or outsourcing. — [4] —. Senior union director Miguel Hayek said he was willing to work with management to safeguard jobs in the face of current uncertainty in the market.

172. What is the article mainly about?

(A) Economic trends in South America
(B) Labor relations at auto companies
(C) Productivity changes in car factories
(D) Ongoing corporate reorganizations

173. The word "subsidiary" in paragraph 2, line 6, is closest in meaning to

(A) divisional
(B) remaining
(C) partial
(D) sequential

174. What problem is Diaz Motors facing?

(A) A lack of competitive technologies
(B) Sharp decreases in stock prices
(C) A reduction of market share
(D) A slump in consumer demand

175. In which of the positions marked [1], [2], [3] and [4] does the following sentence best belong?

"The news comes as the Mexican car manufacturer battles a regional recession."

(A) [1]
(B) [2]
(C) [3]
(D) [4]

GO ON TO THE NEXT PAGE

🚗 Car4U Inc.

C u s t o m e r   S u r v e y

Customer Name: (Mr.)/Ms.) _Ibrahim Rafsanjani_

Address: _17 Rue De Mons, Lyons, France 90A-E7K_

E-mail: _Rafsanjani2947@francotel.com_

Date of Car Rental: From _8 June_ to _15 June_

Applicable rules, fees or other information regarding your rental: _N/A_

Please indicate your level of service satisfaction with Car4U Inc. by rating us in each of the categories below, from _1_ to _5_.   1= Very unsatisfied   5 = Very satisfied

Category	Condition of car at time of rental	Cost per day	Service Staff Helpfulness	Car Model Options	Drop-off and Pick-up convenience
Rating	4	3	3	1	3

Comments: _I think my responses above show my opinion about renting from you. I have also rented from Falcon Rental Co., and frankly I believe they do a better job. It's easy to see why they're the number one car rental agency in Europe. I would recommend that you work to improve your service if you want to compete with them._

Thank you for taking the time to fill out our survey. Fully completed surveys earn 200 Frequent Flier Miles on World Wings Airlines. Let World Wings fly you across the globe—and choose Car4U when you land.

```
* E-mail *                                                    ✕
```

From:	eva.veblen@car4u.net
To:	robert.heller@car4u.net
Date:	18 July
Subject:	Survey

Dear Mr. Heller,

We completed a survey of customer satisfaction last month: over 3,000 respondents were included. I have a broad statistical analysis of the results I will send later. However, I have attached this particular response because the scores are representative of many of the surveys we collected. Furthermore, the respondent offered a succinct written summary of what other customers might also feel.

As you can see, it indicates that we have varying levels of performance in different areas. I spoke with some analysts in the company who said it is "impossible" to perform well in all areas.

However, I don't accept this as necessarily true. Instead, I would like to suggest that we try to make improvements in our worst area of performance, clearly shown in the survey, by expanding our budget in that area. I know that it's not easy to increase expenses, but in my opinion it would be a very positive move that would result in the long-term success of our company.

Yours truly,

Eva Veblen
Director of Operations

176. What is Mr. Rafsanjani most satisfied with?

(A) The state of the cars
(B) Rental fees
(C) The quality of customer service
(D) Car models available

177. Why does Mr. Rafsanjani mention Falcon Rental Co.?

(A) To provide a comparison
(B) To comment on a car he rented
(C) To support his comments on price
(D) To complain about the company's service

178. What do people who answer the survey get?

(A) Lower rental prices
(B) Complimentary airline upgrades
(C) Frequent flier miles
(D) Discounted accommodations

179. Why did Ms. Veblen attach the single response?

(A) It answers her boss' request.
(B) It is a good example of the overall survey results.
(C) It corrects a previous statistical error.
(D) It solicits approval for more responses.

180. What does Ms. Veblen suggest doing to improve the company's performance?

(A) Conducting market research
(B) Cutting down on labor expenses
(C) Increasing the variety of cars
(D) Analyzing the results of the survey

GO ON TO THE NEXT PAGE

www.cheshirefoods.com/raspberryleaftea/

Thank you for visiting Cheshire Foods. See our <u>main Internet homepage</u> for exciting links to other great Cheshire products.

A delicate blend of raspberry leaf, natural flavor and real pieces of apple comes together to make this deliciously fragrant tea.
Completely organic, without artificial flavorings, colors or preservatives.

What's inside?

Raspberry Leaves, Hibiscus, Blackberry Leaves, Natural Raspberry Flavor, Tartaric Acid, Rosehips, Raspberries, Apple pieces.
CAFFEINE-FREE

How to enjoy it?

Place the teabag in a cup or teapot of boiled water (one bag per person). Immerse for 3-5 minutes to bring out the full flavor. Best drunk without adding milk, cream or any other liquids or condiments.

Unfortunately, we are unable to make direct sales.
Please pick up some at your local grocery store.

* E-mail * ✕

To:	CustomerService@Cheshirefoods.com
From:	gloria7902@laketel.com
Date:	Wednesday, May 3
Subject:	Ordering raspberry tea

Dear Cheshire Foods,

I have enjoyed your Raspberry Leaf Tea for many years. I usually take mine with a bit of Korean or Chinese ginseng, and find it delicious. I even check for product updates regularly on your Web site.

Indeed, I think it would be ideal if I were able to buy it there directly. That's because I sometimes forget to pick it up when I'm out shopping. At other times, your tea may not be available at a particular store I go to. In such cases, I purchase other products, though they are not as enjoyable as yours.

Is there any way that I could order directly from your company—perhaps by catalog or phone? If you have no way for customers to do so at this time, I suggest you consider making such an option available. You would certainly benefit through increased sales, and customers like me would benefit through the convenience of the product being brought right to our doors. I should tell you that Longfellow Grey Tea does provide such a service already.

Sincerely,

Gloria Han

---

181. What is a stated feature of Cheshire Foods Raspberry Leaf Tea?

(A) Low price
(B) New flavors
(C) Natural ingredients
(D) Wide popularity

182. What suggestion does the Web site offer?

(A) To add apple pieces to the tea
(B) To allow to cool before consuming
(C) To use the appropriate type of teapot
(D) To avoid adding any dairy products

183. What is indicated about Ms. Han?

(A) She enjoys tea in a different way from the producer's instructions.
(B) She prefers ginseng to raspberry leaf tea.
(C) She purchases tea in large quantities.
(D) She goes shopping for tea at a certain store.

184. What does Ms. Han ask Cheshire Foods to do?

(A) Post product updates on their Web site
(B) Provide product details
(C) Use larger tea boxes
(D) Increase their products' availability

185. How does Ms. Han try to persuade Cheshire Foods to consider her suggestion?

(A) By mentioning a competitor
(B) By threatening to shop elsewhere
(C) By illustrating a business mistake
(D) By showing past losses

GO ON TO THE NEXT PAGE ➡

Starden Foods, Inc.

Created by Consumer Research Department
June 29

Comparison of marketing expenses on food categories with sales changes

Study covered all 637 stores in the European Union. A comparison next quarter will focus on stores in the Americas and the Asia Pacific.

Department	Amount spent on marketing (in millions)	Change in unit sales from last year
Fruits and Vegetables	€4.3	+4.2%
Breads	€12.8	+3.8%
Dry Goods	€26.6	-1.9%
Meats	€18.2	+0.5%
Dairy	€31.4	-2.2%
Seafood	€12.6	+0.1%

Note: Scheduled for discussion at the Marketing Plans Meeting on July 25. There will be an updated schedule soon.

Starden Foods, Inc.

Division Manager Committee Meetings for the Month of July

Final agendas for each meeting will be issued at least 3 days ahead of time. Attendance at all meetings is mandatory, unless urgent client-related or other business arises.

Date	Topic
July 4	Supplier Review
July 11	Marketing Plans
July 18	Store Maintenance Issues
July 25	Quality Control
July 31	Human Resources

Board directors may attend any meeting with little or no advance notice.

> **MEMO**
>
> To: Division Managers
> From: Brenda Phan, COO
> Date: July 12
> Subject: Business Report
>
> Colleagues,
>
> In yesterday's meeting, we discussed whether there is a correlation between the amount of money spent on marketing certain products and the revenue generated from those products. Currently, we can say that the connection is not very clear. We reviewed the list that compares shopper spending traits, and found some surprises. Helen Smith had to miss the meeting, but we talked afterwards. She pointed out products that experienced high sales growth.
>
> You might intuitively feel that we have to spend more money on our products experiencing the lowest sales. However, I think it would be better instead to increase marketing support for our products experiencing the highest sales.
>
> If a product category is experiencing weak sales, I do not think that more advertising alone can improve the situation. Instead, we have to look at other factors, such as quality or price. That is what I tried to stress to Evan Lee, who unexpectedly but fortunately was able to join the meeting. He seemed to agree with my analysis. In any event, I have attached a report detailing this idea, which I'd like to discuss at our next meeting. I don't think that we should put it off until the last gathering of the month.
>
> Thank you,
>
> Brenda Phan

186. According to the list, what is true about the research?

(A) It compares different shopper categories.
(B) It spans several quarters.
(C) It includes many Asian stores.
(D) It covers a single region.

187. What is suggested about the list?

(A) It was created by an outside firm.
(B) It will be distributed at a meeting.
(C) A meeting about it was rescheduled.
(D) A report about it has been written.

188. What is indicated about the July 11 meeting?

(A) A member had urgent business.
(B) A rule was revised.
(C) A maintenance issue was solved.
(D) An important client was invited.

189. In the memo, the word "connection" in paragraph 1, line 3, is closest in meaning to

(A) termination
(B) wire
(C) relationship
(D) payment

190. Who most likely is Evan Lee?

(A) A marketing expert
(B) A senior executive
(C) A consumer analyst
(D) A dairy manufacturer

GO ON TO THE NEXT PAGE ➡

H-3000 Mobile Phone

This best-selling device is easy to use to surf the Web, download apps, talk, text, and perform many other functions. Its most valuable feature is its ability to link to wireless systems even in remote locations.

The device is only compatible with Karn Telecom hardware. This extends to chargers, power cords, and batteries.

A product warranty is enclosed, covering all internal components for 3 years. External surfaces and damage from dropping or ordinary wear and tear are excluded.

---

www.electronicshopper.net/reviews/892361/

Customer comment

Product: The H-3000 Mobile Phone
Customer: Blake Woods
Verified Purchase:

I can say that the device is basically good. I enjoy it in most respects. The price is a little high, and the design isn't particularly elegant, but it does have excellent reception, just as advertised. I am very pleased with that.

I was disappointed, however, because the screen scratched too easily—after only a month of use. I took it to a Karn Telecom store, but the Customer Service representative there only cited the warranty information. In my opinion, the company should reevaluate what "ordinary wear and tear" means.

Customer comment

www.electronicshopper.net/reviews/892361/

Product: The H-3000 Mobile Phone
Customer: Blake Woods
Response from: Karn Telecom Customer Service

Thank you very much for your review. Your feedback is very important to us. Unfortunately, our 3-year warranty is explicit on the subject of surface wear, and the response given to you by the Customer Service representative you spoke with is consistent with that. However, if you do opt for a replacement, we recommend our Z-1X model, which has a stronger screen and is more scratch-resistant. Additionally, we would suggest enrolling in our Extended Care Program. This will warranty your internal components for 2 additional years. The cost for this program is only $175. We want to make sure that you receive the very best support for your product, and we look forward to your continued patronage and feedback.

---

191. What is NOT mentioned in the product information?

(A) Internet use
(B) Access security
(C) Battery components
(D) Sales ranking

192. In the online review, the word "respects" in paragraph 1, line 1, is closest in meaning to

(A) predictions
(B) transmissions
(C) aspects
(D) patterns

193. What is Mr. Woods particularly pleased with about the mobile phone?

(A) Its connectivity
(B) Its compatibility
(C) Its design
(D) Its price

194. What is the total warranty length Karn Telecom can offer?

(A) 1 year
(B) 3 years
(C) 4 years
(D) 5 years

195. What was the Customer Service representative correct about?

(A) The method to avoid scratches
(B) The need for program enrollment
(C) The coverage for a device
(D) The best kind of mobile phone screen

GO ON TO THE NEXT PAGE ➡

Jowel Community Center
17 Lakeland Street
www.jowelccenter.org

Special Event: Building Your Wealth — Tips for Ordinary People
Speaker: Joseph Steinz, Personal Financial Consultant
April 23

Free and open to the public

Learn: Home budget management skills
Choosing the right bank or financial institution
The basics of stocks, bonds, and other investing or reinvesting options

30-Minute Question and Answer Session to follow the talk
Tea, coffee and snacks provided

While the event is free and open to the public, space is limited, and guaranteed seating can be assured only to the first 75 people who register. Please visit the Web site above to register. For more information, contact Bozena Kovac, special event organizer: bozena@jowelccenter.org.

---

* E-mail *	
To:	bozena@jowelccenter.org
From:	joseph.steinz@zoneumail.net
Date:	April 11
Subject:	Second Reminder: Certification

Dear Ms. Kovac,

I regret to inform you that I will not be able to speak at your April 23 Community Center event on finance management. I have an urgent business matter that I have to attend to on that day. I do not want to let down your attendees, so I have arranged a colleague of mine to take my place. I can guarantee that he is more than qualified to do so as he has both taught and written extensively on this topic. Details are in the attachment.

I apologize for this situation, and trust the event will work out well. If I can help in any other way, please do not hesitate to let me know.

Yours sincerely,

Joseph Steinz

NEWS DAILY

Special Event at Jowel Community Center

By Eve Sanders, Special Correspondent

It was a pleasure to hear Wazir Sanjrani speak at the April 23 financial planning event at the Jowel Community Center. This highly accomplished investor took complex topics such as stocks, bonds, and mutual funds, and simplified them so that everyone could understand. He did this repeatedly and in a friendly way, making the talk not only informative but pleasant.

He also explained clearly how people could slowly grow their money starting with just a low sum. This was encouraging, since most of the attendees were simple working men and women. I think all of the attendees also appreciated the fact that Mr. Sanjrani allowed a full one-hour question and answer session.

However, I believe the audiovisual system of the center could benefit from renovation. Several times, it faded out and it was difficult to understand what the speaker was saying.

196. What information is NOT mentioned in the notice?

(A) Photo IDs
(B) Participant registration
(C) Refreshment items
(D) Event location

197. What is indicated about Wazir Sanjrani?

(A) He updated a Web site.
(B) He earned speaker fees.
(C) He works at a bank.
(D) He replaced a presenter.

198. What is indicated about the event?

(A) The main topic of the session was changed.
(B) The payment to sign up was increased.
(C) Entrance to the location was unrestricted.
(D) The question and answer time was extended.

199. In the article, what does Ms. Sanders say the speaker did well?

(A) He summarized his financial accomplishments.
(B) He reviewed the best financial markets.
(C) He put difficult topics into plain terms.
(D) He made individual investment portfolios.

200. What problem is mentioned in the article?

(A) Attendees were fewer than expected.
(B) Some equipment was defective.
(C) Some topics were omitted.
(D) Financial analyses were unclear.

Stop! This is the end of the test. If you finish before time is called, you may go back to Parts 5, 6, and 7 and check your work.

第二回
全真測驗

Model Test 2

* 聽力部分的錄音內容從 MP3 059 開始。
* 答案卡置於本書末，請自行撕下使用。

LISTENING TEST

The Listening test allows you to demonstrate your ability to understand spoken English. The Listening test has four parts, and you will hear directions for each of them. The entire Listening test is approximately forty-five minutes long. Write only on your answer sheet, not the test book.

PART 1

Directions: For each question in PART 1, you will hear four statements about a picture. Choose the statement that best describes what you see in the picture and mark your answer on the answer sheet. The statements will be spoken only once, and do not appear in the test book.

Statement (C), "They are wearing glasses," is the best description of the picture, so you should mark (C) on your answer sheet.

1.

2.

GO ON TO THE NEXT PAGE

3.

4.

5.

6.

GO ON TO THE NEXT PAGE ➤

PART 2

Directions: In PART 2, you will hear either a statement or a question and three responses. They will be spoken only once, and do not appear in your test book. Choose the best response to the question or statement and mark the corresponding letter (A), (B), or (C) on your answer sheet.

7. Mark your answer on your answer sheet.

8. Mark your answer on your answer sheet.

9. Mark your answer on your answer sheet.

10. Mark your answer on your answer sheet.

11. Mark your answer on your answer sheet.

12. Mark your answer on your answer sheet.

13. Mark your answer on your answer sheet.

14. Mark your answer on your answer sheet.

15. Mark your answer on your answer sheet.

16. Mark your answer on your answer sheet.

17. Mark your answer on your answer sheet.

18. Mark your answer on your answer sheet.

19. Mark your answer on your answer sheet.

20. Mark your answer on your answer sheet.

21. Mark your answer on your answer sheet.

22. Mark your answer on your answer sheet.

23. Mark your answer on your answer sheet.

24. Mark your answer on your answer sheet.

25. Mark your answer on your answer sheet.

26. Mark your answer on your answer sheet.

27. Mark your answer on your answer sheet.

28. Mark your answer on your answer sheet.

29. Mark your answer on your answer sheet.

30. Mark your answer on your answer sheet.

31. Mark your answer on your answer sheet.

PART 3

Directions: In PART 3, you will hear several short conversations between two or more people. After each conversation, you will be asked to answer three questions about what you heard. Choose the best response to each question, and mark the corresponding letter (A), (B), (C), or (D) on your answer sheet. The conversations do not appear in the test book, and they will be spoken only one time.

32. Where are the speakers?

(A) In Dublin
(B) In London
(C) In Brussels
(D) In Paris

33. What does the woman want Michelle to do?

(A) Send her an e-mail
(B) Call her directly
(C) Fax her some files
(D) Come to see her

34. What does one of the men say will happen in a few minutes?

(A) A conference will end.
(B) A train will leave.
(C) A deadline will arrive.
(D) A project will be launched.

35. Who most likely is the woman?

(A) A tour agent
(B) An airline clerk
(C) A bank representative
(D) An insurance salesperson

36. What would the man prefer to take on his trip?

(A) A debit card
(B) A credit card
(C) Cash
(D) Traveler's checks

37. What does the SunCrest logo on ATMs and buildings indicate?

(A) The brand is popular.
(B) The usage fee is low.
(C) Debit cards can be used.
(D) The machine is new.

38. Where most likely are the speakers?

(A) On an airplane
(B) On a bus
(C) On a ship
(D) On a train

39. What is the final destination?

(A) Philadelphia
(B) Boston
(C) New York
(D) Washington, D.C.

40. When is the woman likely to reach her destination?

(A) In about two hours
(B) In about three hours
(C) In about four hours
(D) In about five hours

41. Where most likely are the speakers?

(A) At a conference
(B) At a presentation
(C) At a workplace
(D) At a library

42. What will happen on June 25?

(A) New employees will start work.
(B) A department will relocate.
(C) Presentations will end.
(D) Training will begin.

43. What must the speakers do today?

(A) Alter the program schedule
(B) Verify attendance
(C) Hand in their brochures
(D) Go to a conference

GO ON TO THE NEXT PAGE ➡

44. What is the woman doing?

(A) Returning goods
(B) Concluding a transaction
(C) Applying for credit
(D) Explaining about products

45. How much did the woman save?

(A) 10 percent
(B) 20 percent
(C) 25 percent
(D) 30 percent

46. What did the woman misunderstand?

(A) The credit card limit
(B) The item price
(C) The location of the store
(D) The refund policy

47. What are the speakers mainly discussing?

(A) Expanding their market share
(B) Offering a discount
(C) Lowering expenses
(D) Selling new products

48. Why does the man think that they need to change their supplier?

(A) To access better materials
(B) To remain competitive
(C) To order online
(D) To raise product prices

49. What did Ricardo do?

(A) Transferred to eastern Europe
(B) Simplified operations
(C) Saved money
(D) Reviewed the data

50. What most likely is the Red Wolf?

(A) A radio
(B) A mobile phone
(C) A Web site
(D) A television set

51. What does the man offer to do for the woman?

(A) Exchange a model
(B) Upgrade a component
(C) Show her some products
(D) Order a product

52. Why does the woman say, "the simpler, the better"?

(A) She does not need a lot of extra functions.
(B) She wants to acquire the product promptly.
(C) She values unique design features.
(D) She strongly believes in quality over quantity.

53. Where most likely are the speakers?

(A) At an amusement park
(B) At a bus terminal
(C) At a movie theater
(D) At a bookstore

54. What is the woman's preferred time?

(A) 1:00
(B) 3:00
(C) 7:00
(D) 10:00

55. What does the man suggest the woman do?

(A) Wait for two hours
(B) Check another area
(C) Get a refund
(D) Accept an alternative

56. What are the speakers doing?

(A) Touring a site
(B) Preparing for an event
(C) Taking a break
(D) Making a presentation

57. What does the woman mean when she says, "I think I'd rather not"?

(A) She is not interested in the exhibition.
(B) She hopes that she will quit her job soon.
(C) She wants to stay and work in the office.
(D) She might be able to accompany the man.

58. What will the attendees receive?

(A) Presents
(B) Complimentary tickets
(C) Gift certificates
(D) Conference brochures

---

59. What happened last night?

(A) A door was installed.
(B) A system was changed.
(C) An entrance was closed.
(D) A code was updated.

60. What does the man say about the woman's ID card?

(A) It needs a new magnetic strip.
(B) It needs to be replaced.
(C) It works when slid through a reader.
(D) It works at another entrance.

61. Why does the man recommend seeing Susan?

(A) She supervises human resources.
(B) She manages IT.
(C) She makes repairs.
(D) She has more details.

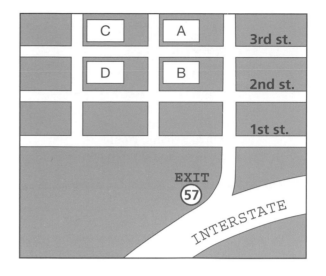

62. What is probably the woman's problem?

(A) She has lost some documents.
(B) She cannot find a location.
(C) She has to change plans quickly.
(D) She does not have a car.

63. What is the man being asked to do?

(A) Attend a meeting
(B) Travel downtown
(C) Clean an office
(D) Sign some papers

64. Look at the graphic. Where is the downtown branch office located?

(A) Building A
(B) Building B
(C) Building C
(D) Building D

GO ON TO THE NEXT PAGE ➡

STYLE #55xl-navy

100% COTTON

||||||||||||||||||||||||||||||||||||

Dry clean or machine
wash cold. Inside out
with like colors. Tumble
dry low. Non-chlorine
bleach only.

Made in U.S.A.

L

$16.99

Candie's Candleworks

$4 Jar Candles
Buy One, Get One FREE

Present this coupon to receive one jar
candle of equal or lesser value with the
purchase of one at regular price.
Must be presented at time of purchase.
Limit one coupon per customer.

65. What is the conversation mainly about?

(A) An incorrect purchase
(B) Overpayment for an item
(C) A problem with an item
(D) An item being out of stock

66. Look at the graphic. How could the problem
have been avoided?

(A) By using cold water
(B) By using hot water
(C) By using bleach
(D) By drying the item

67. What does the woman suggest the man do?

(A) Buy a different size
(B) Wash the item again
(C) Get a refund for the item
(D) Purchase another item

68. What is the woman's problem?

(A) She cannot use a coupon.
(B) She does not have enough money.
(C) She cannot find an item.
(D) She cannot get a refund.

69. Look at the graphic. How many free candles
will the woman get?

(A) Two
(B) Three
(C) Four
(D) Six

70. What will the man most likely do next?

(A) Contact another store
(B) Wrap some items
(C) Take a customer's order
(D) Look for another candle

PART 4

Directions: In PART 4, you will hear several short talks. After each talk, you will be asked to answer three questions about what you heard. Choose the best response to each question, and mark the corresponding letter (A), (B), (C), or (D) on your answer sheet. The questions and responses are printed in the test book. The talks do not appear in the test book, and they will be spoken only one time.

71. According to the speaker, what can be found in the training materials?

(A) Locations of all the divisions
(B) Names of their competitors
(C) Information about the company's expertise
(D) Advice on investments

72. What is implied about Leighton?

(A) It has gained a large market share.
(B) It has existed for a long time.
(C) It has used complex strategies.
(D) It has recruited new managers.

73. What will the listeners do next?

(A) Take off their ID badges
(B) Retrieve their mobile phones
(C) Go up to the second floor
(D) Tour the trading area

74. What is the advertisement mainly about?

(A) A product demonstration
(B) A travel opportunity
(C) A local competition
(D) A sales campaign

75. What feature of Lemon Gold One Gel is mentioned?

(A) Size
(B) Popularity
(C) Usefulness
(D) Price

76. What does the speaker imply when he says, "Seats will be given on a first come, first served basis"?

(A) There are no more seats left.
(B) People should come to the place early.
(C) The show will start earlier than planned.
(D) A light meal will be given during the show.

77. What is the report mainly about?

(A) An upcoming takeover
(B) An appointment of a new CEO
(C) An upturn in consumer spending
(D) New markets in China

78. What will the companies achieve as a result of the deal?

(A) Higher revenue
(B) Better products
(C) Reduced costs
(D) Improved technologies

79. According to the report, what has been Mr. Rice's policy at Astar Pharmaceuticals?

(A) Increasing size
(B) Upgrading services
(C) Raising share prices
(D) Production in mainland China

80. What does the speaker imply when she says, "I can barely hear music on it, no matter which direction I turn the dial"?

(A) There is something wrong with the volume dial.
(B) The directions are too complicated for her.
(C) She cannot find the dial to turn.
(D) She wants to know what music is on.

81. What does the speaker want to do?
(A) Find a manual
(B) Extend a warranty
(C) Locate a repair shop
(D) Receive a new product

82. What does the speaker say about herself?
(A) She has had the same problem before.
(B) She has made partial repairs.
(C) She has called previously.
(D) She has received a replacement.

GO ON TO THE NEXT PAGE

第2回全真測驗

PART 3/4

83. What is the main purpose of the talk?

(A) To announce a schedule
(B) To perform a new opera
(C) To outline a goal
(D) To discuss problems

84. According to the speaker, how many euros have been donated so far?

(A) 2.0 million
(B) 2.1 million
(C) 2.2 million
(D) 2.3 million

85. What is an advantage of being a sponsor?

(A) Music previews
(B) Backstage passes
(C) Free champagne
(D) Exclusive events

86. Who most likely are the listeners?

(A) Corporate staff
(B) Business journalists
(C) Media analysts
(D) Market regulators

87. What is Richard Kashumbe's current occupation?

(A) Marketing manager
(B) Film director
(C) Communication expert
(D) Journalist

88. What will happen next?

(A) Refreshments will be served.
(B) A different speaker will talk.
(C) A press conference will begin.
(D) Questions will be taken.

89. Why does the woman say, "Yes, you heard right"?

(A) To agree with an opinion
(B) To emphasize what she says
(C) To ask for permission
(D) To show her gratitude

90. What is true of the goods in Aisle 3?

(A) They are from major companies.
(B) They are unique to Victoria Supermarket.
(C) They are all edible.
(D) They are sold only in the morning.

91. What are customers using Aisle 3 unable to do?

(A) Pay by credit cards
(B) Buy leading brands
(C) Receive shopping points
(D) Shop in other aisles

92. What is the broadcast mainly about?

(A) Financial results
(B) Leadership changes
(C) Brand development
(D) Market trends

93. What is Bob Heller expected to do next?

(A) Leave the company
(B) Hire a rival
(C) Transfer to Toronto
(D) Oversee investments

94. What has Jason Yu said he will do?

(A) Increase net income
(B) Raise staffing levels
(C) Lower manufacturing costs
(D) Launch new products

Johnson Corp.

Maintenance Request Form

Submitted by: ___Royce Brown___

Supervisor: ___Michael Halvorsen___

Location: ___Meeting Room 4___

Room Setup

- 70 chairs, 7 rows of 10

- Set up projector screen on west side
  of room

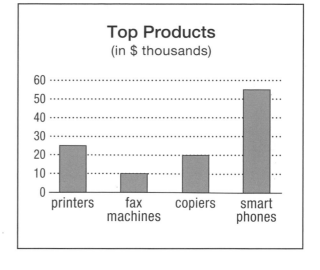

Top Products
(in $ thousands)

printers | fax machines | copiers | smart phones

95. Why is the woman calling?

(A) To cancel an order
(B) To amend a request
(C) To make an appointment
(D) To schedule a meeting

96. Look at the graphic. What does the woman want Mike to do before the meeting?

(A) Put the screen on the east side of the room
(B) Move some tables to the other room
(C) Reduce the number of chairs
(D) Change the type of projector

97. When will Mike most likely return the call?

(A) This morning
(B) This afternoon
(C) Tomorrow morning
(D) Tomorrow afternoon

98. Where most likely does the man work?

(A) At a printing company
(B) At an office supply retailer
(C) At a research firm
(D) At a telecommunications center

99. Look at the graphic. What figure does the man predict as a result of the campaign?

(A) $20,000
(B) $30,000
(C) $40,000
(D) $50,000

100. What will the man do after the meeting?

(A) Help with a campaign
(B) Put together a report
(C) Make a presentation
(D) Consult with a department

This is the end of the Listening test. Turn to Part 5 in your test book.

GO ON TO THE NEXT PAGE ➡

第2回全真測驗

PART 4

READING TEST

In the Reading part of the test, you will read several different types of texts and answer a variety of questions. The Reading test has three parts, and directions are provided for each of them. You will have seventy-five minutes to complete the entire Reading test. Answer as many questions as you can within the time allotted. Write only on your answer sheet, not the test book.

PART 5

Directions: There is a word or phrase missing from each of the sentences below. Following each sentence are four answer choices: (A), (B), (C), and (D). Choose the answer that best completes the sentence and mark that letter on your answer sheet.

101. Heart Life Corporation's new medicine will be distributed in pharmacies after ------- over a period of 18 months certifies that it is safe.

    (A) test
    (B) being tested
    (C) tested
    (D) have tested

102. The entire downtown business area was filled ------- 12 hours with shoppers enjoying holiday discounts.

    (A) as
    (B) in
    (C) on
    (D) for

103. Analysts report that shopping online for groceries has ------- changed the entire supermarket experience.

    (A) dramatically
    (B) accusingly
    (C) impenetrably
    (D) combatively

104. Chinese retailer Zin Mart predicted no ------- in profits for the year, despite a slowdown in consumer spending.

    (A) deteriorate
    (B) deteriorated
    (C) deteriorating
    (D) deterioration

105. In case this event is canceled, ticket holders will each ------- the full face value of their purchase.

    (A) entitle
    (B) receive
    (C) remove
    (D) object

106. Trascki Automobile Company has gone from strength ------- strength since entering the North American market.

    (A) on
    (B) in
    (C) and
    (D) to

107. Millions of consumers are rushing to buy the game software, leaving storeowners ------- to meet demand.

    (A) conflicting
    (B) contesting
    (C) targeting
    (D) struggling

108. The ------- merit of Mr. Rysbecki's financial model comes from its ability to predict demand for the company's products.

    (A) relative
    (B) relation
    (C) relate
    (D) relatively

109. Mr. Kim said he would prefer ------- in the Seoul office rather than transfer to the smaller branch in Incheon.

(A) remains
(B) to remain
(C) remained
(D) had remained

110. CEO Gawande of IndoOne Tech was known for his honest and ------- approach to business negotiations.

(A) opening
(B) openly
(C) open
(D) opened

111. The client ------- us make several revisions to the advertising campaign literature, such as putting the logo in a more prominent position.

(A) had
(B) did
(C) permitted
(D) got

112. Harris Corporation acted ------- in recruiting the very best personnel for all of its divisions.

(A) assertion
(B) asserting
(C) asserts
(D) assertively

113. Green World Foods emerged as the most ------- brand in a survey, with 93% of respondents feeling positive about the company.

(A) imported
(B) trusted
(C) reviewed
(D) assumed

114. The emergence of satellite TV is generating a crucial ------- that even local entertainment companies can market globally.

(A) understands
(B) understandably
(C) understanding
(D) understandable

115. The board of directors at Dragon Robotics Co. reacted ------- to the idea of merging with a rival corporation.

(A) positively
(B) positive
(C) positiveness
(D) positivity

116. Professor Shah's expertise in industrial engineering earned him an ------- reputation in his field.

(A) insurable
(B) unwarranted
(C) unintentional
(D) enviable

117. Director Khan said the senior managers of the company had made a number of ------- comments regarding its reorganization.

(A) construction
(B) constructive
(C) construct
(D) constructively

118. The expansion of Titan Corporation's factories in Indonesia ------- as part of its goal of increasing output from its facilities in the region.

(A) will see
(B) is seeing
(C) was seen
(D) being seen

119. Global Footwear Inc. is ------- larger than its domestic rivals, which gives it a much larger marketing budget.

(A) consecutively
(B) considerably
(C) consequently
(D) confusingly

120. Following months of -------, Joshua Technologies publicly announced its takeover of Carpon Digital Design for £375.5 million.

(A) education
(B) speculation
(C) performance
(D) regulation

GO ON TO THE NEXT PAGE

121. Lopez Telecom Co. won a contract to build a telecommunication network in Eastern Europe, ------- in a 14% rise in profits.

(A) result
(B) to result
(C) resulting
(D) will result

122. The success of the Crystal Mountain Resort Hotel ------- by its low vacancy rate of only about 3% almost year-round.

(A) could determine
(B) can be determined
(C) to be determined
(D) is determining

123. One of the main strengths of Ms. Chou's company lies in ------- ability to uncover previously undeveloped markets.

(A) it
(B) herself
(C) hers
(D) its

124. Attendees at the One Globe Financial Seminar will have a chance to learn ------- corporations should carefully manage their internal cash reserves at all times.

(A) they
(B) why
(C) them
(D) what

125. Organic foods at Happy Face Restaurants are becoming ------- popular, as people realize the benefits of making healthy food choices.

(A) increasing
(B) increase
(C) increasingly
(D) increment

126. Although White Sky Airlines has lost some of its market share in recent years, it is still ------- than its rivals.

(A) establishing
(B) establishes
(C) more established
(D) most established

127. The *Dancing Baby* doll created a great ------- among consumers, and sold in very large numbers upon its initial release.

(A) sensation
(B) compensation
(C) determination
(D) promotion

128. The communications department ------- the company's media coverage, both at home and abroad.

(A) monitors
(B) renovates
(C) contacts
(D) invests

129. PetCare1.com is a corporation ------- has been able to tap into the multibillion dollar pet market by shipping a variety of dog and cat-related products directly to owners.

(A) who
(B) whose
(C) which
(D) what

130. Caris Coffee has ------- its commitment to donate 5% of its annual profits to charities in Eastern Kenya.

(A) confirmed
(B) contributed
(C) contacted
(D) concerned

PART 6

Directions: There is a word, phrase, or sentence is missing from parts of each of the following texts. Below each text, there are four answer choices for each question: (A), (B), (C), and (D). Choose the answer that best completes the text and mark the corresponding letter on your answer sheet.

Questions 131-134 refer to the following e-mail.

To: Francesco Milletti
From: Masoud Akbar
Date: 31 August
Subject: Replacement request

Dear Mr. Milletti,

I received your e-mail yesterday. In it, you ------- the shipment of the construction materials from
    131.
Milan. I have pasted information from that e-mail below.

Steel beams ⋯⋯⋯⋯⋯⋯⋯	200
Wood beams ⋯⋯⋯⋯⋯⋯⋯	175
Concrete mix ⋯⋯⋯⋯⋯⋯	500 kilograms
Glass Panes ⋯⋯⋯⋯⋯⋯⋯	600
Tools ⋯⋯⋯⋯⋯⋯⋯⋯⋯⋯	34 pieces

We have checked the shipment, and most of the goods that arrived are fine. There is one issue,

however: ------- the number of glass panes noted above totaled what we had ordered, there were
        132.
variances in quality. Some of the panes were quite thick, for example, while others were thin.

-------. We would therefore like to have 100 replacement panes ------- to us.
133.   **134.**

If you are able to do this before 7 September, that would be ideal, as that would mean minimum disruption to our construction schedule. Please let me know when we can expect the replacement units.

Regards,
Masoud Akbar

131. (A) confirmed
     (B) negotiated
     (C) permitted
     (D) accepted

132. (A) yet
     (B) despite
     (C) unless
     (D) although

133. (A) We really like these high-quality products.
     (B) We really need all the items to be of a similar quality.
     (C) These panes are normally either too thick or thin.
     (D) There are no complaints whatsoever about the price.

134. (A) send
     (B) sent
     (C) sending
     (D) to send

GO ON TO THE NEXT PAGE

Ajit Rahman
22 Ackley Road
Nashville, TN
December 3

Dear Mr. Rahman,

Please find a recent summary of the ------- on your account below.
                                      135.

Amount in account at start of period: $500,000
Withdrawal, November 13 ....$6,000
Deposit, November 15......................$5,320
Withdrawal, November 30 ....$4,200
Ending Balance: $495,120

We'd also like to remind you that ------- for overdraft protection is highly recommended. Such
                                   136.
protection guards you against fees which would otherwise be incurred.

You are currently eligible for up to $5,000 in overdraft protection. Many of our customers feel that this

provides them with -------, as they know they will not be penalized if they write checks for amounts
                   137.
temporarily not in their accounts. -------.
                                   138.

Sincerely,

Renee Zuiller
Account Manager
r.zuiller@d-bank.com

---

135. (A) upgrades
(B) purchases
(C) transactions
(D) investments

136. (A) applies
(B) applicable
(C) applications
(D) applying

137. (A) secure
(B) secured
(C) more security
(D) more securely

138. (A) Please e-mail me if you are interested in this program.
(B) Please let me know if this is possible at your earliest convenience.
(C) If you have any recommendations, I would like to hear them.
(D) I look forward to receiving your next report soon.

The management at Lysell Corporation ------- staff to take care of their bodies as well as their
139.
careers.

Apart from our company fitness center and health plan, we have recently launched a Healthy Living

campaign, ------- by the Human Resources Department. -------. More precisely, the campaign is
140. **141.**
designed to get our staff to exercise, eat right, and watch their weight. Already, 210 employees have

signed up for it.

Elisabeth Choi from the Human Resources Department, who leads the campaign, recommended

the staff could get in ------- in various ways, such as cycling to work instead of driving, or taking the
142.
stairs instead of the elevators.

139. (A) encouraging
(B) encouragement
(C) encouragingly
(D) encourages

140. (A) contacted
(B) converted
(C) developed
(D) declared

141. (A) However, the campaign has been
running quite smoothly.
(B) The aim of the campaign is to help our
staff improve their well-being.
(C) The communication plan would boost
the campaign's impact.
(D) Therefore, we would appreciate your
contribution to this cause.

142. (A) position
(B) place
(C) touch
(D) shape

GO ON TO THE NEXT PAGE

From: David Martin, Operations Director
To: Luiz Rodriguez, Carmel Falls Manager
Subject: Georgetown Branch Opening
Date: Monday, May 5

Luiz,

As you know, the Georgetown Branch of PizzaMan Inc. is due to open this fall. As a result, we now

need to ------- staff in the local area.
       143.

The Carmel Falls Branch is only 10 miles away, so we would like to offer some of your staff the

opportunity to join ------- there. We feel that their previous experience of working for PizzaMan could
       144.
be extremely important in ------- the new branch a success.
       145.

Please let your employees know about this great new career option as soon as possible. -------.
       146.

Sincerely,

David Martin

---

143. (A) reorganize
    (B) recruit
    (C) outsource
    (D) survey

144. (A) theirs
    (B) us
    (C) our
    (D) their

145. (A) causing
    (B) going
    (C) letting
    (D) making

146. (A) We will give priority to those who have been with us the longest.
    (B) We look forward to serving you at our new Carmel Falls branch.
    (C) This is the very first time we have treated you like this.
    (D) All staff members should report to work on time each day.

PART 7

Directions: PART 7 consists of a number of texts such as e-mails, advertisements, and newspaper articles. After each text or set of texts there are several questions. Choose the best answer to each question and mark the corresponding letter (A), (B), (C), and (D) on your answer sheet.

Questions 147-148 refer to the following ticket.

ADMIT ONE ADULT
Summer of Strings
An evening of classical music with the Singapore National Symphony Orchestra

Kwan Teok Hall
Doors Open: 7:30 P.M.
Performance First Half: 8:15 P.M.
Intermission: 10:00 P.M.
Performance Second Half: 10:30 P.M.

No cameras, videos or other recording devices allowed. No admittance after 10 minutes before the show starts. Please turn off all phones prior to entering. Except in the event of a performance cancellation, all ticket sales are final.

147. When is the latest that ticketed guests may enter to see the performance?

(A) 7:30 P.M.
(B) 8:05 P.M.
(C) 8:15 P.M.
(D) 10:00 P.M.

148. What is stated on the ticket?

(A) Seating may be unreserved.
(B) Refunds are not usually available.
(C) No cancellations are allowed.
(D) Performance dates are limited.

GO ON TO THE NEXT PAGE

Questions 149-150 refer to the following text message chain.

Geordie Jacobsen   May 8, 9:15 A.M.
Hi April, sorry to bother you. I know you're on your way to a client's office. Just curious, do you know if Accounting finished compiling last week's sales figures yet?

April Meeker   May 8, 9:18 A.M.
Yes. Sandra told me. They sent the file to her. I'll text her and have her send it to you by e-mail.

Geordie Jacobsen   May 8, 9:19 A.M.
Great. I was thinking we could include that data in our presentation tomorrow. Newest is best, right?

April Meeker   May 8, 9:21 A.M.
I agree, but ask Accounting first whether it's OK. They have to make the call on that one.

Geordie Jacobsen   May 8, 9:22 A.M.
OK. I'll do that now. I'll message you what they say.

April Meeker   May 8, 9:23 A.M.
Great!

149. What is Ms. Meeker doing now?

(A) Gathering some data
(B) Preparing for a presentation
(C) Writing an e-mail to Accounting
(D) Going to a client's office

150. At 9:21 A.M., what does Ms. Meeker most likely mean when she writes, "They have to make the call on that one"?

(A) Accounting has to give permission to use data.
(B) Accounting has to give a presentation.
(C) She has to make a phone call to Accounting.
(D) She has to forward the data to Mr. Jacobsen.

Annual Pan-Pacific Telecom Association Meeting

Macau Lotus Hotel
Pandora Room
July 7

The Association is pleased to announce that during this year's meeting, a keynote lecture will be given by Mr. Sun Liu Fan, widely regarded as the world's leading authority on global telecommunications. His research has led to the development of new insights on emerging advances in the industry. This has enabled both corporations and government regulators to maximize the benefits of this dynamic field.

Following the release of his latest book, *A World Connected*, Mr. Sun will share his most recent findings on telecommunications in emerging markets.

All those wishing to attend the lecture can get more information at www.panpacifictelecomassoc.net/lectures/.

*Fees for attending the annual meeting are not inclusive of the lecture. Those should be covered in advance through the online address noted above.

151. According to the information, what is Mr. Sun renowned for?

(A) His regulatory authority over markets
(B) His financial investments into industry
(C) His many years of experience in different corporations
(D) His expertise and research in a specific field

152. What will attendees who want to hear the lecture have to do?

(A) Join the Association
(B) E-mail Mr. Sun
(C) Pay an extra charge
(D) Download a pass

GO ON TO THE NEXT PAGE

Questions 153-154 refer to the following instructions.

The Revlar Microwave Oven User Guide

Position your oven away from sources of heat or moisture, for optimum efficiency.

Do not operate it when empty.

Use appropriate, heat-resistant cookware, including knives, forks or spoons, at all times. Keep bowls partially covered while cooking, but never seal them completely.

You may see moisture collecting on the inner walls or the door when the oven is in use. This is normal.

Cooking time varies according to quantity, as well as the fat or water content of the food. Monitor cooking progress to prevent food from drying out, burning or catching fire.

Food with skins or membranes – like whole apples, potatoes or tomatoes – must be pierced before cooking.

Clean the insides of the oven and its door after each use so that it remains perfectly dry. This will prevent corrosion.

153. What is stated about the cookware?

(A) It should be kept away from moisture.
(B) It should not be used in an operating oven.
(C) It should be able to withstand heat.
(D) It should be sealed inside bowls.

154. What is recommended in the instructions?

(A) The oven should be operated when empty.
(B) The food should be dry before cooking.
(C) Airtight containers should be used.
(D) Holes should be poked into some food before cooking.

* E-mail *	✕

From:	Kim Su-mi, Director, Han Kang Construction Corp. KOREA
To:	Fara Suleiman, President, Malaya One Real Estate MALAYSIA
Subject:	Consort Building
Date:	1 August

Dear Ms. Suleiman,

Following our videoconference of 29 July with our architects Franklin & Josephs, we feel it is necessary to visit your office to discuss the ongoing progress of the Consort Building project. We hope 4 August might be acceptable to you.

In your last e-mail, you also mentioned needing our assistance with some of your interior work. As you are aware, our agreement covers only the exterior of the building. However, we can recommend Maxima Space Co., headquartered in Rome. They have extensive experience with interiors, and have worked with us on buildings like yours in the past. Maxima Vice-president Ron Fascenelli has told me his corporation is quite capable of installing carpeting, furnishings, and handling painting for each of the 273 offices within the office building, in addition to other decorating needs as may be required.

I have taken the liberty of asking Mr. Fascenelli to send you a brochure package about his company by post. You can also learn more about them through their Web site www. maximaspaceitalia.com or simply e-mailing Mr. Fascenelli at ron.f@maximaspace.com.

We hope this helps you in your situation.

Yours sincerely,

Kim Su-mi

155. What is the purpose of Ms. Kim's upcoming meeting with Ms. Suleiman?

(A) To meet construction architects
(B) To propose additional project outlines
(C) To provide updates on construction work
(D) To inspect building specifications

156. Why does Ms. Kim recommend Maxima Space Co.?

(A) They have developed many building exteriors.
(B) They dominate the market in Rome.
(C) They have done a lot of work in interior projects.
(D) They offer the lowest prices.

157. What does Ms. Suleiman expect to receive soon?

(A) An e-mail from the vice-president
(B) Some reading material from overseas
(C) A phone call regarding construction deadlines
(D) A Web site service agreement

GO ON TO THE NEXT PAGE ▶

Come Join the Team at Symington Company
We Animate the World!

Symington Company, headquartered in New Zealand, announces openings in its Riga, Latvia office.

About us: We are one of the largest companies in the Asia-Pacific region, known for our cutting-edge animation technologies. Our employees are dedicated, hard-working, and generally long-term. Our compensation packages are in most cases well above industry averages. We were chosen "Best Company to Work For" this year by the business news Web site, 21CTrade.com.
Our recent moves: We are now entering the European market. The Riga office is intended to serve as the company's base for the Eastern Europe-Russia region.

We are looking for staff in the following areas:

- **Computer Graphics & Animation**
- **Print Illustration**
- **Information Technologies**
- **Management**

All applicants must have at least 3 years of experience in their respective fields. Managerial applicants must have at least 4 additional years. Medium fluency in English required; medium or advanced fluency in Russian, German or French is preferred.

Those interested in one of the positions listed above may apply online at www.symingtonanimation.com/jobs/animation/latvia/. Callers to Personnel about this position will be directed back to this site. Faxed résumés will receive no response. Interviews will take place from October 5 to October 12 at our Riga headquarters, and those who are selected for positions will be notified by October 20. Most positions will start October 23.

158. What is indicated about Symington Company?

(A) It is well known in the European region.
(B) It is respected for its Web site technologies.
(C) It is famous for its award-winning products.
(D) It is noted for its generosity to its staff.

159. How much experience is required for applicants for managerial positions?

(A) Three years
(B) Four years
(C) Five years
(D) Seven years

160. When will Symington Corporation inform successful candidates?

(A) By October 5
(B) By October 12
(C) By October 20
(D) By October 23

GO ON TO THE NEXT PAGE ➡

Accounting for the New Century —in the Right Way

If your company commonly has errors in its financial reports, the accounting computer network, not the staff, is usually more to blame. — [1] —. The errors themselves are only a symptom of that underlying problem.

Consulting companies can advise you on which accounting computers to purchase. These computers are able to manage very large amounts of data, and are linked to a central network.

— [2] —. Best of all, they commonly have easy to follow operation instructions. Consulting companies can offer advice on using these computers and teach staff to increase productivity through them.

These consulting companies also maintain industry-wide benchmarks for your accounting department. — [3] —. Their Ax Blue reports published each year provide an overview of how corporations and corporate departments in over 200 areas stay world-class. Meeting benchmarks like these ensures that your company is rising to the best practices within your industry. — [4] —.

161. According to the article, why do most accounting errors occur?

(A) Reports are done too quickly.
(B) Companies have insufficient data.
(C) Computer systems are inadequate.
(D) Supervisors lack management skills.

162. How are the Ax Blue reports helpful to corporations?

(A) They list the largest corporations in each field.
(B) They show how to maintain top standards in different sectors.
(C) They showcase the best managers at major businesses.
(D) They provide an overview of important markets.

163. In which of the positions marked [1], [2], [3] and [4] does the following sentence best belong?

"AxTor Consulting Group is a good example of this."

(A) [1]
(B) [2]
(C) [3]
(D) [4]

BLIGO TRADING SERVICES

Friday, July 28

Following the senior directors' meeting last week, it has been decided that structural changes at the Bligo Hong Kong branch are necessary. The following measures are to be implemented to make operations more cost-efficient. These changes will be implemented in stages.

August 1
All help desk issues will be handled by our Bangalore, India global consumer service center. Help desk facilities in Hong Kong, including both human operators and the automated answering system, will cease.

August 20
The human resources department will utilize Web technologies for recruiting, staff management, employee benefits and other staff services to the maximum extent to decrease current costs in the department.

August 31
Personnel from the sales and marketing divisions will merge into one group, with expected staffing reductions of 42%.

While it is regrettable that some of these steps will result in job losses for the departments concerned, we are pleased to announce that several new positions have been created in our Mainland China division. Staff who are interested in applying are urged to contact Lisa Vu at lisa.vu@bligo.net for an application form.

---

164. What is the purpose of the changes being made by Bligo Trading?

(A) To improve facilities
(B) To reduce operating costs
(C) To reward performance
(D) To upgrade services

165. What change is being planned for the human resources department?

(A) Fewer people will be recruited.
(B) Regular work hours will be reduced.
(C) Employee benefits will decrease.
(D) Online systems will be used.

166. What will happen on August 31?

(A) Sales will be emphasized over marketing.
(B) A company merger will occur.
(C) Two departments will be combined.
(D) The size of a group will be increased.

167. The word "concerned" in paragraph 5, line 2, is closest in meaning to

(A) worried
(B) controlled
(C) related
(D) detailed

GO ON TO THE NEXT PAGE

Questions 168-171 refer to the following online chat discussion.

Rex Johnson [3:01 P.M.]
Thanks, everyone, for agreeing to this online session. It's much easier than trying to organize a meeting on such short notice. Now then, could we start with opinions?

Anita Doorn [3:03 P.M.]
Mai, we ran the same number of commercials as always, right?

Mai Yang [3:04 P.M.]
We did. No change from last quarter. I can't figure it out.

Rex Johnson [3:06 P.M.]
We're marketing the same style computer with the same specs as our competitor, Sundry Corp. Still, sales are down for some reason.

Michael Boswell [3:08 P.M.]
Did we get any customer feedback from the surveys?

Abdullah Farooq [3:09 P.M.]
Yes, we got some. We haven't reviewed them thoroughly yet, but I saw a number of comments referencing Sundry.

Rex Johnson [3:10 P.M.]
Really? That's news to me. That probably means their publicity is better.

Joe Forbes [3:11 P.M.]
We should look into that immediately. I'll do some Internet research, and I'll ask around and see what I can find out.

Mai Yang [3:12 P.M.]
Good idea. Any information would help. If I know what Sundry is doing, I can get the ball rolling on production of a new commercial.

---

168. What is the reason for the discussion?

(A) To discuss a commercial
(B) To review sales figures
(C) To analyze a customer survey
(D) To solicit input from staff

169. What most likely is Ms. Yang's job in the company?

(A) She oversees advertisements.
(B) She builds computer applications.
(C) She designs Web pages.
(D) She manages sales.

170. At 3:10 P.M., what does Mr. Johnson most likely mean when he writes, "That's news to me"?

(A) He was unaware.
(B) He was misinformed.
(C) He wants to tell more people.
(D) He wants to contact the media.

171. According to the discussion, what most likely will happen next?

(A) Customer feedback will be received.
(B) Sales will go up.
(C) A new commercial will be reviewed.
(D) A company will be researched.

Science-M Contest

Sponsored by Suvar Corporation
Islamabad, Pakistan

Are you the next great scientist to come out of Pakistan?

Suvar Corporation is sponsoring a nationwide campaign to find the next generation of young geniuses from our country.

Top Prize: A full 4-year scholarship to the university of your choice anywhere within the nation. — [1] —.

Second Place: A set of 10 software educational packages from Suvar Corporation.

Third Place: Gift certificates for use at department stores in Lahore, Islamabad, Karachi and other major cities.

Here is how you can compete against the best young minds in Pakistan.

To enter the contest, you must be over 12 and under 20.* — [2] —. Entrants may submit any original creation within the following areas:

- **Robotics**
- **Software**
- **Biotech**
- **Hardware**
- **Pharmaceuticals**

All submissions must be entirely the work of the entrant, without any assistance from teachers, parents or other adults. — [3] —. If an entrant wishes to work with classmates on a submission, it must then be clearly labeled as teamwork.

The deadline for registering submissions is June 15. — [4] —. Entry inspections by a panel of judges will begin June 18, with a final winner chosen June 21.

*While anyone within this age group can compete, most top prizes in past years have usually gone to those aged between 17 and 19.

---

172. What is the stated purpose of the Science-M Contest?

(A) To find marketable technical products
(B) To improve business research capabilities
(C) To help fund educational programs
(D) To discover talented people

173. Which is NOT listed as a gift for prize winners?

(A) Coupons for goods
(B) Educational materials
(C) Fees for tuition
(D) Travel tickets

174. What rule is mentioned about the contest?

(A) Group work must be specified.
(B) Adult assistance is encouraged.
(C) Registration fees are required.
(D) Submissions require teacher approval.

175. In which of the positions marked [1], [2], [3] and [4] does the following sentence best belong?

"While not necessary, a strong background in science is preferred."

(A) [1]
(B) [2]
(C) [3]
(D) [4]

GO ON TO THE NEXT PAGE

June 17

Project Coordinator

Orange Tech Co

Orange Tech is the largest telecom company in our regional markets. Recently, we were awarded a contract for the construction of satellite broadcasting systems throughout the Republic of South Africa.

To cope with this increased workload, we are searching for a reliable project coordinator to assist the operations manager in charge of this task.

Candidates must have a minimum of a BA degree, with a graduate degree preferred. They must have at least three years' experience in the field, and be able to demonstrate excellent interpersonal skills.

Knowledge of the following software applications is required:
- **TX25**
- **InfoScoop**
- **Arcana**
- **IsoFin**

Regular duties will include database management, compilation of weekly reports, installation schedule development, and resolution of any outstanding technical issues.

Please submit credentials by July 9 to Adam De Groot at the following address, adam.degroot@orangetech.za

```
┌─────────────────────────────────────────────────────────────┐
│                        * E-mail *                        [×] │
├─────────────────────────────────────────────────────────────┤
│ To:       adam.degroot@orangetech.za                         │
│ From:     darren.zimbele@africatel.com                       │
│ Date:     Wednesday, June 20                                 │
│ Subject:  Open Position                                      │
└─────────────────────────────────────────────────────────────┘
```

Attachments: References.doc
　　　　　　 CV.doc

Dear Mr. De Groot,

I am writing about your project coordinator position.

I graduated from Keele University, with an MSc in computer engineering two years ago. Since then, I have worked in Kampala Tech Co. as a software analyst, first in their Kimberly and Pretoria branches and now here in Johannesburg. There, I gained extensive experience working with TX25, InfoScoop, Arcana, IsoFin, and many other software packages.

Beyond my technical background, I also get on well with all sorts of people. Even while under the stress of tight work deadlines, I never get angry or frustrated.

I look forward to hearing from you soon.

Sincerely,

Darren Zimbelc

176. What will Orange Tech require their new recruit to do?

(A) Manage a new project
(B) Get a new contract
(C) Expand into a new market
(D) Acquire a new company

177. In the notice, the word "interpersonal" in paragraph 3, line 3, is closest in meaning to

(A) profitable
(B) communicative
(C) academic
(D) linguistic

178. Where does Mr. Zimbele currently work?

(A) Cape Town
(B) Kimberly
(C) Pretoria
(D) Johannesburg

179. What can be inferred about Mr. Zimbele from his application?

(A) He does not have enough work experience.
(B) He does not have the required academic background.
(C) He does not have sufficient references.
(D) He does not have adequate software skills.

180. Why does Mr. Zimbele mention deadlines?

(A) To emphasize his attention to details
(B) To highlight his computer skills
(C) To show his leadership background
(D) To demonstrate his patience

GO ON TO THE NEXT PAGE →

Branson Lawn & Garden Co.
We make the exterior of every home a lovely one.

Lawn care	**Garden care**
Bush, tree and hedge trimming	**Special services as required**

Deposits accepted but not required.
Handling both commercial and residential projects. Our clients include:

- *XSoft Computer Corporation*
- *Briar City Park*
- *Leviston Apartment Complex*
- *And homes all over the city*

Our Management Team:

Linda Wu —————— President
linda.wu@bransononline.com

Armando Benitez —— Personnel manager
armando.b@bransononline.com

Mary Listz —————— Client Project manager
mary.l@bransononline.com

Frank Cole —————— Equipment manager
frank.cole@bransononline.com

Voted Number 1 Landscaping Service by City Life Magazine

Drop by our office
at 302 Beckridge Way
or contact us at:
info@bransononline.com.

You'll be glad you did!

*On the job seven days a week, through all four seasons. All work done from November 1 through April 1 requires additional fees.

E-mail

From:	michelle017@northtel.com
To:	linda.wu@bransononline.com
Date:	Monday, May 25
Subject:	Your Company

Dear Ms. Wu,

Thank you for taking the time to talk with me on the phone earlier today. After doing so, I think I might be interested in hiring your company for some landscaping projects around my home. Ordinarily, I enjoy taking care of my yard and garden on weekends, but I'm so busy at the office nowadays it's hard for me to devote as much time to it as I used to.

I think that if you carried out the work we discussed for me every fourteen days, I could keep the greenery around my home looking good. So I'd like to start with that sort of schedule. However, weekly visits might be required during spring, when everything grows very fast. If your company also does snow removal, I might also have monthly work for you in winter, or more frequently according to the snowfall.

I understand you will be sending out one of your managers tomorrow who is responsible for customer cost estimates. During that meeting I would like to discuss the service contract, including all labor, equipment and other factors. I would prefer a complete total of that in your estimate, rather than being surprised later by unanticipated prices.

Best regards,

Michelle Walker

181. What is implied about Branson Lawn & Garden Co.?

(A) It accepts online payments.
(B) It offers big discounts.
(C) It has a good reputation.
(D) It does interiors as well as exteriors.

182. What is stated about Branson Lawn & Garden Co.?

(A) It serves only corporate clients.
(B) It requires a deposit before beginning work.
(C) It limits projects during some seasons.
(D) It charges more during certain periods.

183. How often does Ms. Walker want initial service?

(A) Every week
(B) Every other week
(C) Every month
(D) Every other month

184. Who will Ms. Walker meet tomorrow?

(A) Linda Wu
(B) Armando Benitez
(C) Mary Listz
(D) Frank Cole

185. What is one request made by Ms. Walker?

(A) Getting a comprehensive quote
(B) Receiving fast performance
(C) Confirming top equipment
(D) Understanding project details

GO ON TO THE NEXT PAGE ➡

October 27

Richard Yeoh
Laxfield Office Supplies Corporation
7861 Clayton Plaza
Denver, CO 98775

Dear Mr. Yeoh,

I was sorry to hear that your stay at our hotel in Portland, Oregon, was less than satisfactory. You should not have had your seminars exposed to the noise from work crews renovating our lobby and main entrance. I understand that at many points your presenters struggled to be heard because of that.

Unfortunately, when taking your reservation for the Premier Gold Room, our receptionist made a mistake by overlooking the fact that it was adjacent to the areas under renovation. As a Sunshine Hotels Card member, you are entitled to nothing less than top-class service.

To make up for your inconvenience in some small way, I hope that you will accept the voucher enclosed.

With very best regards,

Josef Loos

Josef Loos
Vice President
Sunshine Hotels, Inc.

Sunshine Hotels Inc.

Taking care of you 365 days a year!

Guest Voucher

This voucher entitles the bearer to a 50% discount on our hotels anywhere in the United States or Canada, including our Royal Suite or Deluxe Suite rooms.

Voucher No. A982JQRV08

Expires December 27
Non-transferable, single-use only

Sunshine Hotels Card members receive an additional 10% off. Valid only for online reservations at www.sunshinehotels/vouchers/. Please enter voucher number noted above.

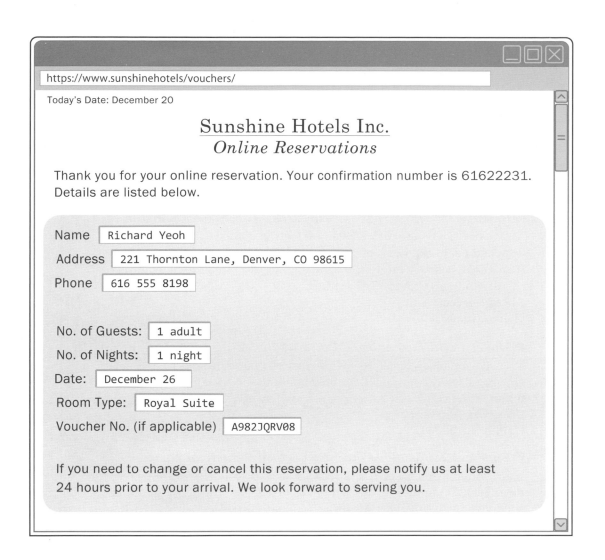

https://www.sunshinehotels/vouchers/

Today's Date: December 20

Sunshine Hotels Inc.
Online Reservations

Thank you for your online reservation. Your confirmation number is 61622231. Details are listed below.

Name Richard Yeoh

Address 221 Thornton Lane, Denver, CO 98615

Phone 616 555 8198

No. of Guests: 1 adult

No. of Nights: 1 night

Date: December 26

Room Type: Royal Suite

Voucher No. (if applicable) A982JQRV08

If you need to change or cancel this reservation, please notify us at least 24 hours prior to your arrival. We look forward to serving you.

---

186. What is the purpose of the letter?

(A) To confirm a reservation
(B) To explain facilities
(C) To reply to an inquiry
(D) To make an apology

187. What problem occurred at the seminars?

(A) Baggage was not delivered.
(B) Speakers could not be heard.
(C) Locations were changed.
(D) Presentations were rescheduled.

188. In the letter, the word "way" in paragraph 3, line 1, is closest in meaning to

(A) manner
(B) condition
(C) payment
(D) portion

189. What is the maximum discount available to Mr. Yeoh?

(A) 10%
(B) 50%
(C) 60%
(D) 70%

190. What is indicated about Mr. Yeoh?

(A) He had seminars at a hotel near his office.
(B) He reserved the wrong room for the seminars.
(C) He will stay at a Sunshine Hotel on December 20.
(D) He was given a voucher valid for two months.

GO ON TO THE NEXT PAGE

Thorren Industries

This Week's Top Properties!

Philadelphia, Pennsylvania

■ *Downtown Office Space in Historic Building—18 Winston St.*
Entire 3rd floor (just under 8,000 sq. feet) in gorgeous historic brownstone, in the heart of downtown. Beautifully restored turn-of-the-century interior, but with all modern amenities including air conditioning and computer facilities.
$13.00/sq. feet/year
Listing No. 32330

■ *Modern and Convenient—Portmandieu Mall, 4325 Poplar Way*
Two adjacent showroom properties (about 3,000 sq. feet each) in quiet suburban location, in first-floor-only building. Up-to-date facilities. Just 30 minutes from downtown via expressway, Exit 351.
$13.00/sq. feet/year
Listing No. 32338

■ *Spacious Renovated Warehouse—2000 Industrial Drive*
Huge warehouse building, totally renovated. Easy access to the center of town, just 20 minutes by bus. Total 41,000 sq. feet. Landlord willing to subdivide, will rent space according to tenant needs.
$15.00/sq. feet/year
Listing No. 41323

For inquiries regarding the above properties, please visit our Web site at www.thorrenind.com/inquiries.

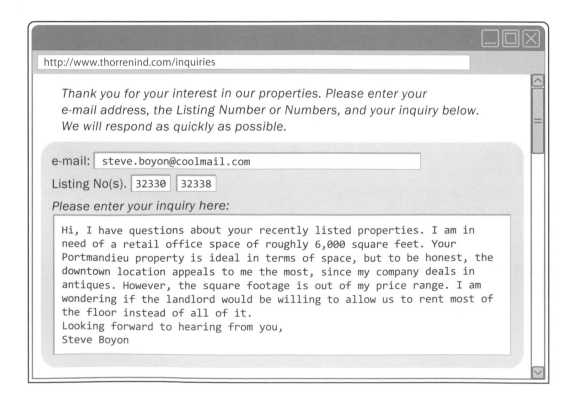

http://www.thorrenind.com/inquiries

Thank you for your interest in our properties. Please enter your e-mail address, the Listing Number or Numbers, and your inquiry below. We will respond as quickly as possible.

e-mail: steve.boyon@coolmail.com
Listing No(s). 32330 32338

Please enter your inquiry here:

Hi, I have questions about your recently listed properties. I am in need of a retail office space of roughly 6,000 square feet. Your Portmandieu property is ideal in terms of space, but to be honest, the downtown location appeals to me the most, since my company deals in antiques. However, the square footage is out of my price range. I am wondering if the landlord would be willing to allow us to rent most of the floor instead of all of it.
Looking forward to hearing from you,
Steve Boyon

```
┌─────────────────────────────────────────────────────────────────────────┐
│                              * E-mail *                              [×]  │
├──────────┬────────────────────────────────────────────────────────────────┤
│ To:      │ steve.boyon@coolmail.com                                       │
├──────────┼────────────────────────────────────────────────────────────────┤
│ From:    │ anetta.fasiq@thorrenreal.com                                   │
├──────────┼────────────────────────────────────────────────────────────────┤
│ Date:    │ May 12                                                         │
├──────────┼────────────────────────────────────────────────────────────────┤
│ Subject: │ Listing No. 32330                                              │
└──────────┴────────────────────────────────────────────────────────────────┘
```

Dear Mr. Boyon,

Thank you for your interest in this property. We have contacted the landlord, Mr. John Fedder. Unfortunately, he has informed us that the property cannot be subdivided. However, he commented that he has spent a lot of time and money having the building restored, and seemed delighted by the nature of your business. He has graciously offered to negotiate a better price per square foot. If this is of interest to you, please contact me via e-mail, or by phone at (612) 555-8181. I will contact him immediately and arrange for you to meet as soon as possible.

Regards,

Anetta Fasiq

191. What most likely does Thorren Industries specialize in?

(A) Retail merchandising
(B) Real estate
(C) Building renovation
(D) Construction

192. What is the purpose of Mr. Boyon's inquiry?

(A) To negotiate a lower price
(B) To complete a lease
(C) To ask about rental terms
(D) To give feedback on a property listing

193. What does Mr. Boyon indicate about the property on Poplar Way?

(A) The space is ideal.
(B) It is too expensive for him.
(C) It is not conveniently located.
(D) It does not have adequate facilities.

194. What is implied about Mr. Fedder?

(A) He is fond of antiques.
(B) He specializes in renovation.
(C) He can rent out parts of his property.
(D) He has contacted Mr. Boyon.

195. In the e-mail, what does Ms. Fasiq say she can do for Mr. Boyon?

(A) Help reduce the rental price
(B) Accelerate the rental process
(C) Recommend a different property
(D) Renovate some facilities

GO ON TO THE NEXT PAGE →

X Cola Consumers. Survey Responses
by Age Group (DRAFT 1)

Age Group	Number of Responses
20-29	705
30-39	142
40-49	117
50+	51

Hansen Food & Beverage Corporation
X-Cola Market Research Team
Julia Arbenz, Team Leader

Note to Eric: Here's the first draft of the slide for the presentation on Wednesday, for your review. Please e-mail me as soon as possible with any feedback. Thanks! — Julia

---

∗ E-mail ∗

To:	Julia Arbenz <j.arbenz@x-cola.com>
From:	Eric Bradshaw <eric.b@x-cola.com>
Date:	January 14, 11:56 A.M.
Subject:	Consumer data, first draft

Hi Julia,

Thanks for your hard work. At a glance, the data doesn't look that different from last year's. First, it might be good to make the table into a chart. Also, this year, could we add data for consumers between the ages of 13 and 19? In other words, teenagers, but we can label this group "young adults."

The reason I ask is, our senior staff have already proposed diverting more money to ad campaigns for people 30 and over, but personally I'm a little hesitant to concur with that idea.

If you have any survey data on young adults, would you send it to me, as well as your thoughts? I'd appreciate both.

Thanks,

Eric Bradshaw
Marketing Director, Hansen Food & Beverage

> *** E-mail ***

To:	Eric Bradshaw \<eric.b@x-cola.com\>
From:	Julia Arbenz \<j.arbenz@x-cola.com\>
Date:	January 14, 1:02 P.M.
Subject:	Re: Consumer data, first draft

Hi Eric,

I just checked the data you requested. Surprisingly, the number of responses was even lower than the 50+ age group in the survey results I sent in the first draft.

However, that might be because teenagers simply don't bother to return as many surveys as people in older age brackets. So, in actuality, the number of teenage consumers might be greater.

In any event, from a research perspective, I am inclined to side with your opinion. If you would like me to convey that to the senior staff, please let me know. I'll be sending you an updated slide momentarily.

Best wishes,

Julia

196. What most likely is Julia's job position?

(A) Team assistant
(B) Senior manager
(C) IT specialist
(D) Marketing analyst

197. What is indicated about the number of teenage consumer responses?

(A) It is significantly small.
(B) It has increased proportionally.
(C) It is the same as last year.
(D) It is as was expected.

198. What does Julia imply about ad campaign money?

(A) It should be spent on ads for younger people.
(B) It has already been raised by her team.
(C) It is sufficient for more ads to be made.
(D) More funding is needed for further research.

199. In the second e-mail, the word "brackets" in paragraph 2, line 2, is closest in meaning to

(A) lengths
(B) ranges
(C) differences
(D) targets

200. What does Julia say she will do next?

(A) Reexamine the data
(B) Contact senior staff
(C) Call Eric
(D) Provide a new slide

Stop! This is the end of the test. If you finish before time is called, you may go back to Parts 5, 6, and 7 and check your work.

做完模擬試題並對完答案之後，請參考下表將正解數換算成分數，以預測正式考試時的得分。本表格與 TOEIC 測驗的分數計算方式無關，僅供推測目前實力之用。

第一回全真測驗

聽力

正解數	預測分數	正解數	預測分數	正解數	預測分數
100	495	69	390	38	235
99	495	68	385	37	230
98	495	67	380	36	225
97	495	66	375	35	220
96	495	65	370	34	215
95	490	64	365	33	210
94	490	63	360	32	205
93	490	62	355	31	200
92	485	61	350	30	195
91	485	60	345	29	190
90	480	59	340	28	185
89	480	58	335	27	180
88	475	57	330	26	175
87	475	56	325	25	170
86	470	55	320	24	165
85	470	54	315	23	160
84	465	53	310	22	155
83	460	52	305	21	150
82	455	51	300	20	145
81	450	50	295	19	140
80	445	49	290	18	135
79	440	48	285	17	130
78	435	47	280	16	125
77	430	46	275	15	120
76	425	45	270	14	115
75	420	44	265	13	110
74	415	43	260	12	105
73	410	42	255	11	100
72	405	41	250	~10	無法測定
71	400	40	245		
70	395	39	240		

閱讀

正解數	預測分數	正解數	預測分數	正解數	預測分數
100	495	69	385	38	230
99	495	68	380	37	225
98	490	67	375	36	220
97	490	66	370	35	215
96	485	65	365	34	210
95	485	64	360	33	205
94	485	63	355	32	200
93	480	62	350	31	195
92	480	61	345	30	190
91	480	60	340	29	185
90	475	59	335	28	180
89	475	58	330	27	175
88	470	57	325	26	170
87	470	56	320	25	165
86	465	55	315	24	160
85	465	54	310	23	155
84	460	53	305	22	150
83	455	52	300	21	145
82	450	51	295	20	140
81	445	50	290	19	135
80	440	49	285	18	130
79	435	48	280	17	125
78	430	47	275	16	120
77	425	46	270	15	115
76	420	45	265	14	110
75	415	44	260	13	105
74	410	43	255	12	100
73	405	42	250	~11	無法測定
72	400	41	245		
71	395	40	240		
70	390	39	235		

正解數 /分	+	正解數 /分	=	/分
聽力		閱讀		預測分數

第二回全真測驗

聽力

正解數	預測分數	正解數	預測分數	正解數	預測分數
100	495	69	395	38	240
99	495	68	390	37	235
98	495	67	385	36	230
97	495	66	380	35	225
96	495	65	375	34	220
95	490	64	370	33	215
94	490	63	365	32	210
93	490	62	360	31	205
92	485	61	355	30	200
91	485	60	350	29	195
90	485	59	345	28	190
89	480	58	340	27	185
88	480	57	335	26	180
87	475	56	330	25	175
86	475	55	325	24	170
85	470	54	320	23	165
84	470	53	315	22	160
83	465	52	310	21	155
82	460	51	305	20	150
81	455	50	300	19	145
80	450	49	295	18	140
79	445	48	290	17	135
78	440	47	285	16	130
77	435	46	280	15	125
76	430	45	275	14	120
75	425	44	270	13	115
74	420	43	265	12	110
73	415	42	260	11	105
72	410	41	255	10	100
71	405	40	250	~9	無法測定
70	400	39	245		

閱讀

正解數	預測分數	正解數	預測分數	正解數	預測分數
100	495	69	390	38	235
99	495	68	385	37	230
98	495	67	380	36	225
97	490	66	375	35	220
96	490	65	370	34	215
95	485	64	365	33	210
94	485	63	360	32	205
93	485	62	355	31	200
92	480	61	350	30	195
91	480	60	345	29	190
90	480	59	340	28	185
89	475	58	335	27	180
88	475	57	330	26	175
87	470	56	325	25	170
86	470	55	320	24	165
85	465	54	315	23	160
84	465	53	310	22	155
83	460	52	305	21	150
82	455	51	300	20	145
81	450	50	295	19	140
80	445	49	290	18	135
79	440	48	285	17	130
78	435	47	280	16	125
77	430	46	275	15	120
76	425	45	270	14	115
75	420	44	265	13	110
74	415	43	260	12	105
73	410	42	255	11	100
72	405	41	250	~10	無法測定
71	400	40	245		
70	395	39	240		

正解數 [　　/　分]
聽力

＋

正解數 [　　/　分]
閱讀

＝

[　　/　分]
預測分數

MP3 音軌內容

　　音軌 001-058 收錄第一回聽力測驗的題目，音軌 059-116 收錄第二回聽力測驗題目，音軌 ex01-ex16 則收錄應考要領內的聽力例題和商英字彙。詳細音軌編號之對應內容，請參考下表。

Track 001-058（第一回全真測驗）

MP3	內容	MP3	內容
1	Part 1 Direction	43	No.56~58
2	No.1	44	No.59~61
3	No.2	45	No.62~64
4	No.3	46	No.65~67
5	No.4	47	No.68~70
6	No.5	48	Part 4 Direction
7	No.6	49	No.71~73
8	Part 2 Direction	50	No.74~76
9	No.7	51	No.77~79
10	No.8	52	No.80~82
11	No.9	53	No.83~85
12	No.10	54	No.86~88
13	No.11	55	No.89~91
14	No.12	56	No.92~94
15	No.13	57	No.95~97
16	No.14	58	No.98~100
17	No.15		
18	No.16		
19	No.17		
20	No.18		
21	No.19		
22	No.20		
23	No.21		
24	No.22		
25	No.23		
26	No.24		
27	No.25		
28	No.26		
29	No.27		
30	No.28		
31	No.29		
32	No.30		
33	No.31		
34	Part 3 Direction		
35	No.32~34		
36	No.35~37		
37	No.38~40		
38	No.41~43		
39	No.44~46		
40	No.47~49		
41	No.50~52		
42	No.53~55		

Track 059-116（第二回全真測驗）
Track ex01-ex16（應考要領）

MP3	內容	MP3	內容
59	Part 1 Direction	101	No.56~58
60	No.1	102	No.59~61
61	No.2	103	No.62~64
62	No.3	104	No.65~67
63	No.4	105	No.68~70
64	No.5	106	Part 4 Direction
65	No.6	107	No.71~73
66	Part 2 Direction	108	No.74~76
67	No.7	109	No.77~79
68	No.8	110	No.80~82
69	No.9	111	No.83~85
70	No.10	112	No.86~88
71	No.11	113	No.89~91
72	No.12	114	No.92~94
73	No.13	115	No.95~97
74	No.14	116	No.98~100
75	No.15		
76	No.16		

MP3	內容
ex01	應考要領_Part 1_No.1
ex02	應考要領_Part 1_No.2
ex03	應考要領_Part 1_No.3
ex04	應考要領_Part 2_No.1
ex05	應考要領_Part 2_No.2
ex06	應考要領_Part 2_No.3
ex07	應考要領_Part 3_No.1~3
ex08	應考要領_Part 4_No.1~3
ex09	應考要領_詞彙單元 1
ex10	應考要領_詞彙單元 2
ex11	應考要領_詞彙單元 3
ex12	應考要領_詞彙單元 4
ex13	應考要領_詞彙單元 5
ex14	應考要領_詞彙單元 6
ex15	應考要領_詞彙單元 7
ex16	應考要領_詞彙單元 8

MP3	內容
77	No.17
78	No.18
79	No.19
80	No.20
81	No.21
82	No.22
83	No.23
84	No.24
85	No.25
86	No.26
87	No.27
88	No.28
89	No.29
90	No.30
91	No.31
92	Part 3 Direction
93	No.32~34
94	No.35~37
95	No.38~40
96	No.41~43
97	No.44~46
98	No.47~49
99	No.50~52
100	No.53~55

ANSWER SHEET

Admission No.

NAME

LISTENING TEST (PART 1-4)

#	A B C D	#	A B C D	#	A B C D	#	A B C D
1	Ⓐ Ⓑ Ⓒ Ⓓ	21	Ⓐ Ⓑ Ⓒ	41	Ⓐ Ⓑ Ⓒ Ⓓ	81	Ⓐ Ⓑ Ⓒ Ⓓ
2	Ⓐ Ⓑ Ⓒ Ⓓ	22	Ⓐ Ⓑ Ⓒ	42	Ⓐ Ⓑ Ⓒ Ⓓ	82	Ⓐ Ⓑ Ⓒ Ⓓ
3	Ⓐ Ⓑ Ⓒ Ⓓ	23	Ⓐ Ⓑ Ⓒ	43	Ⓐ Ⓑ Ⓒ Ⓓ	83	Ⓐ Ⓑ Ⓒ Ⓓ
4	Ⓐ Ⓑ Ⓒ Ⓓ	24	Ⓐ Ⓑ Ⓒ	44	Ⓐ Ⓑ Ⓒ Ⓓ	84	Ⓐ Ⓑ Ⓒ Ⓓ
5	Ⓐ Ⓑ Ⓒ Ⓓ	25	Ⓐ Ⓑ Ⓒ	45	Ⓐ Ⓑ Ⓒ Ⓓ	85	Ⓐ Ⓑ Ⓒ Ⓓ
6	Ⓐ Ⓑ Ⓒ Ⓓ	26	Ⓐ Ⓑ Ⓒ	46	Ⓐ Ⓑ Ⓒ Ⓓ	86	Ⓐ Ⓑ Ⓒ Ⓓ
7	Ⓐ Ⓑ Ⓒ Ⓓ	27	Ⓐ Ⓑ Ⓒ	47	Ⓐ Ⓑ Ⓒ Ⓓ	87	Ⓐ Ⓑ Ⓒ Ⓓ
8	Ⓐ Ⓑ Ⓒ Ⓓ	28	Ⓐ Ⓑ Ⓒ	48	Ⓐ Ⓑ Ⓒ Ⓓ	88	Ⓐ Ⓑ Ⓒ Ⓓ
9	Ⓐ Ⓑ Ⓒ Ⓓ	29	Ⓐ Ⓑ Ⓒ	49	Ⓐ Ⓑ Ⓒ Ⓓ	89	Ⓐ Ⓑ Ⓒ Ⓓ
10	Ⓐ Ⓑ Ⓒ Ⓓ	30	Ⓐ Ⓑ Ⓒ	50	Ⓐ Ⓑ Ⓒ Ⓓ	90	Ⓐ Ⓑ Ⓒ Ⓓ
11	Ⓐ Ⓑ Ⓒ Ⓓ	31	Ⓐ Ⓑ Ⓒ	51	Ⓐ Ⓑ Ⓒ Ⓓ	91	Ⓐ Ⓑ Ⓒ Ⓓ
12	Ⓐ Ⓑ Ⓒ Ⓓ	32	Ⓐ Ⓑ Ⓒ	52	Ⓐ Ⓑ Ⓒ Ⓓ	92	Ⓐ Ⓑ Ⓒ Ⓓ
13	Ⓐ Ⓑ Ⓒ Ⓓ	33	Ⓐ Ⓑ Ⓒ	53	Ⓐ Ⓑ Ⓒ Ⓓ	93	Ⓐ Ⓑ Ⓒ Ⓓ
14	Ⓐ Ⓑ Ⓒ Ⓓ	34	Ⓐ Ⓑ Ⓒ	54	Ⓐ Ⓑ Ⓒ Ⓓ	94	Ⓐ Ⓑ Ⓒ Ⓓ
15	Ⓐ Ⓑ Ⓒ Ⓓ	35	Ⓐ Ⓑ Ⓒ	55	Ⓐ Ⓑ Ⓒ Ⓓ	95	Ⓐ Ⓑ Ⓒ Ⓓ
16	Ⓐ Ⓑ Ⓒ Ⓓ	36	Ⓐ Ⓑ Ⓒ	56	Ⓐ Ⓑ Ⓒ Ⓓ	96	Ⓐ Ⓑ Ⓒ Ⓓ
17	Ⓐ Ⓑ Ⓒ Ⓓ	37	Ⓐ Ⓑ Ⓒ	57	Ⓐ Ⓑ Ⓒ Ⓓ	97	Ⓐ Ⓑ Ⓒ Ⓓ
18	Ⓐ Ⓑ Ⓒ Ⓓ	38	Ⓐ Ⓑ Ⓒ	58	Ⓐ Ⓑ Ⓒ Ⓓ	98	Ⓐ Ⓑ Ⓒ Ⓓ
19	Ⓐ Ⓑ Ⓒ Ⓓ	39	Ⓐ Ⓑ Ⓒ	59	Ⓐ Ⓑ Ⓒ Ⓓ	99	Ⓐ Ⓑ Ⓒ Ⓓ
20	Ⓐ Ⓑ Ⓒ Ⓓ	40	Ⓐ Ⓑ Ⓒ	60	Ⓐ Ⓑ Ⓒ Ⓓ	100	Ⓐ Ⓑ Ⓒ Ⓓ

READING TEST (PART 5-7)

#	A B C D	#	A B C D	#	A B C D	#	A B C D
101	Ⓐ Ⓑ Ⓒ Ⓓ	121	Ⓐ Ⓑ Ⓒ Ⓓ	141	Ⓐ Ⓑ Ⓒ Ⓓ	181	Ⓐ Ⓑ Ⓒ Ⓓ
102	Ⓐ Ⓑ Ⓒ Ⓓ	122	Ⓐ Ⓑ Ⓒ Ⓓ	142	Ⓐ Ⓑ Ⓒ Ⓓ	182	Ⓐ Ⓑ Ⓒ Ⓓ
103	Ⓐ Ⓑ Ⓒ Ⓓ	123	Ⓐ Ⓑ Ⓒ Ⓓ	143	Ⓐ Ⓑ Ⓒ Ⓓ	183	Ⓐ Ⓑ Ⓒ Ⓓ
104	Ⓐ Ⓑ Ⓒ Ⓓ	124	Ⓐ Ⓑ Ⓒ Ⓓ	144	Ⓐ Ⓑ Ⓒ Ⓓ	184	Ⓐ Ⓑ Ⓒ Ⓓ
105	Ⓐ Ⓑ Ⓒ Ⓓ	125	Ⓐ Ⓑ Ⓒ Ⓓ	145	Ⓐ Ⓑ Ⓒ Ⓓ	185	Ⓐ Ⓑ Ⓒ Ⓓ
106	Ⓐ Ⓑ Ⓒ Ⓓ	126	Ⓐ Ⓑ Ⓒ Ⓓ	146	Ⓐ Ⓑ Ⓒ Ⓓ	186	Ⓐ Ⓑ Ⓒ Ⓓ
107	Ⓐ Ⓑ Ⓒ Ⓓ	127	Ⓐ Ⓑ Ⓒ Ⓓ	147	Ⓐ Ⓑ Ⓒ Ⓓ	187	Ⓐ Ⓑ Ⓒ Ⓓ
108	Ⓐ Ⓑ Ⓒ Ⓓ	128	Ⓐ Ⓑ Ⓒ Ⓓ	148	Ⓐ Ⓑ Ⓒ Ⓓ	188	Ⓐ Ⓑ Ⓒ Ⓓ
109	Ⓐ Ⓑ Ⓒ Ⓓ	129	Ⓐ Ⓑ Ⓒ Ⓓ	149	Ⓐ Ⓑ Ⓒ Ⓓ	189	Ⓐ Ⓑ Ⓒ Ⓓ
110	Ⓐ Ⓑ Ⓒ Ⓓ	130	Ⓐ Ⓑ Ⓒ Ⓓ	150	Ⓐ Ⓑ Ⓒ Ⓓ	190	Ⓐ Ⓑ Ⓒ Ⓓ
111	Ⓐ Ⓑ Ⓒ Ⓓ	131	Ⓐ Ⓑ Ⓒ Ⓓ	151	Ⓐ Ⓑ Ⓒ Ⓓ	191	Ⓐ Ⓑ Ⓒ Ⓓ
112	Ⓐ Ⓑ Ⓒ Ⓓ	132	Ⓐ Ⓑ Ⓒ Ⓓ	152	Ⓐ Ⓑ Ⓒ Ⓓ	192	Ⓐ Ⓑ Ⓒ Ⓓ
113	Ⓐ Ⓑ Ⓒ Ⓓ	133	Ⓐ Ⓑ Ⓒ Ⓓ	153	Ⓐ Ⓑ Ⓒ Ⓓ	193	Ⓐ Ⓑ Ⓒ Ⓓ
114	Ⓐ Ⓑ Ⓒ Ⓓ	134	Ⓐ Ⓑ Ⓒ Ⓓ	154	Ⓐ Ⓑ Ⓒ Ⓓ	194	Ⓐ Ⓑ Ⓒ Ⓓ
115	Ⓐ Ⓑ Ⓒ Ⓓ	135	Ⓐ Ⓑ Ⓒ Ⓓ	155	Ⓐ Ⓑ Ⓒ Ⓓ	195	Ⓐ Ⓑ Ⓒ Ⓓ
116	Ⓐ Ⓑ Ⓒ Ⓓ	136	Ⓐ Ⓑ Ⓒ Ⓓ	156	Ⓐ Ⓑ Ⓒ Ⓓ	196	Ⓐ Ⓑ Ⓒ Ⓓ
117	Ⓐ Ⓑ Ⓒ Ⓓ	137	Ⓐ Ⓑ Ⓒ Ⓓ	157	Ⓐ Ⓑ Ⓒ Ⓓ	197	Ⓐ Ⓑ Ⓒ Ⓓ
118	Ⓐ Ⓑ Ⓒ Ⓓ	138	Ⓐ Ⓑ Ⓒ Ⓓ	158	Ⓐ Ⓑ Ⓒ Ⓓ	198	Ⓐ Ⓑ Ⓒ Ⓓ
119	Ⓐ Ⓑ Ⓒ Ⓓ	139	Ⓐ Ⓑ Ⓒ Ⓓ	159	Ⓐ Ⓑ Ⓒ Ⓓ	199	Ⓐ Ⓑ Ⓒ Ⓓ
120	Ⓐ Ⓑ Ⓒ Ⓓ	140	Ⓐ Ⓑ Ⓒ Ⓓ	160	Ⓐ Ⓑ Ⓒ Ⓓ	200	Ⓐ Ⓑ Ⓒ Ⓓ

Note: columns 161–180 also present:

#	A B C D
161	Ⓐ Ⓑ Ⓒ Ⓓ
162	Ⓐ Ⓑ Ⓒ Ⓓ
163	Ⓐ Ⓑ Ⓒ Ⓓ
164	Ⓐ Ⓑ Ⓒ Ⓓ
165	Ⓐ Ⓑ Ⓒ Ⓓ
166	Ⓐ Ⓑ Ⓒ Ⓓ
167	Ⓐ Ⓑ Ⓒ Ⓓ
168	Ⓐ Ⓑ Ⓒ Ⓓ
169	Ⓐ Ⓑ Ⓒ Ⓓ
170	Ⓐ Ⓑ Ⓒ Ⓓ
171	Ⓐ Ⓑ Ⓒ Ⓓ
172	Ⓐ Ⓑ Ⓒ Ⓓ
173	Ⓐ Ⓑ Ⓒ Ⓓ
174	Ⓐ Ⓑ Ⓒ Ⓓ
175	Ⓐ Ⓑ Ⓒ Ⓓ
176	Ⓐ Ⓑ Ⓒ Ⓓ
177	Ⓐ Ⓑ Ⓒ Ⓓ
178	Ⓐ Ⓑ Ⓒ Ⓓ
179	Ⓐ Ⓑ Ⓒ Ⓓ
180	Ⓐ Ⓑ Ⓒ Ⓓ

ANSWER SHEET

Admission No.

NAME

LISTENING TEST (PART 1-4)

#		#		#		#		#	
1	Ⓐ Ⓑ Ⓒ Ⓓ	21	Ⓐ Ⓑ Ⓒ	41	Ⓐ Ⓑ Ⓒ Ⓓ	61	Ⓐ Ⓑ Ⓒ Ⓓ	81	Ⓐ Ⓑ Ⓒ Ⓓ
2	Ⓐ Ⓑ Ⓒ Ⓓ	22	Ⓐ Ⓑ Ⓒ	42	Ⓐ Ⓑ Ⓒ Ⓓ	62	Ⓐ Ⓑ Ⓒ Ⓓ	82	Ⓐ Ⓑ Ⓒ Ⓓ
3	Ⓐ Ⓑ Ⓒ Ⓓ	23	Ⓐ Ⓑ Ⓒ	43	Ⓐ Ⓑ Ⓒ Ⓓ	63	Ⓐ Ⓑ Ⓒ Ⓓ	83	Ⓐ Ⓑ Ⓒ Ⓓ
4	Ⓐ Ⓑ Ⓒ Ⓓ	24	Ⓐ Ⓑ Ⓒ	44	Ⓐ Ⓑ Ⓒ Ⓓ	64	Ⓐ Ⓑ Ⓒ Ⓓ	84	Ⓐ Ⓑ Ⓒ Ⓓ
5	Ⓐ Ⓑ Ⓒ Ⓓ	25	Ⓐ Ⓑ Ⓒ	45	Ⓐ Ⓑ Ⓒ Ⓓ	65	Ⓐ Ⓑ Ⓒ Ⓓ	85	Ⓐ Ⓑ Ⓒ Ⓓ
6	Ⓐ Ⓑ Ⓒ Ⓓ	26	Ⓐ Ⓑ Ⓒ	46	Ⓐ Ⓑ Ⓒ Ⓓ	66	Ⓐ Ⓑ Ⓒ Ⓓ	86	Ⓐ Ⓑ Ⓒ Ⓓ
7	Ⓐ Ⓑ Ⓒ	27	Ⓐ Ⓑ Ⓒ	47	Ⓐ Ⓑ Ⓒ Ⓓ	67	Ⓐ Ⓑ Ⓒ Ⓓ	87	Ⓐ Ⓑ Ⓒ Ⓓ
8	Ⓐ Ⓑ Ⓒ	28	Ⓐ Ⓑ Ⓒ	48	Ⓐ Ⓑ Ⓒ Ⓓ	68	Ⓐ Ⓑ Ⓒ Ⓓ	88	Ⓐ Ⓑ Ⓒ Ⓓ
9	Ⓐ Ⓑ Ⓒ	29	Ⓐ Ⓑ Ⓒ	49	Ⓐ Ⓑ Ⓒ Ⓓ	69	Ⓐ Ⓑ Ⓒ Ⓓ	89	Ⓐ Ⓑ Ⓒ Ⓓ
10	Ⓐ Ⓑ Ⓒ	30	Ⓐ Ⓑ Ⓒ	50	Ⓐ Ⓑ Ⓒ Ⓓ	70	Ⓐ Ⓑ Ⓒ Ⓓ	90	Ⓐ Ⓑ Ⓒ Ⓓ
11	Ⓐ Ⓑ Ⓒ	31	Ⓐ Ⓑ Ⓒ	51	Ⓐ Ⓑ Ⓒ Ⓓ	71	Ⓐ Ⓑ Ⓒ Ⓓ	91	Ⓐ Ⓑ Ⓒ Ⓓ
12	Ⓐ Ⓑ Ⓒ	32	Ⓐ Ⓑ Ⓒ	52	Ⓐ Ⓑ Ⓒ Ⓓ	72	Ⓐ Ⓑ Ⓒ Ⓓ	92	Ⓐ Ⓑ Ⓒ Ⓓ
13	Ⓐ Ⓑ Ⓒ	33	Ⓐ Ⓑ Ⓒ	53	Ⓐ Ⓑ Ⓒ Ⓓ	73	Ⓐ Ⓑ Ⓒ Ⓓ	93	Ⓐ Ⓑ Ⓒ Ⓓ
14	Ⓐ Ⓑ Ⓒ	34	Ⓐ Ⓑ Ⓒ	54	Ⓐ Ⓑ Ⓒ Ⓓ	74	Ⓐ Ⓑ Ⓒ Ⓓ	94	Ⓐ Ⓑ Ⓒ Ⓓ
15	Ⓐ Ⓑ Ⓒ	35	Ⓐ Ⓑ Ⓒ	55	Ⓐ Ⓑ Ⓒ Ⓓ	75	Ⓐ Ⓑ Ⓒ Ⓓ	95	Ⓐ Ⓑ Ⓒ Ⓓ
16	Ⓐ Ⓑ Ⓒ	36	Ⓐ Ⓑ Ⓒ	56	Ⓐ Ⓑ Ⓒ Ⓓ	76	Ⓐ Ⓑ Ⓒ Ⓓ	96	Ⓐ Ⓑ Ⓒ Ⓓ
17	Ⓐ Ⓑ Ⓒ	37	Ⓐ Ⓑ Ⓒ	57	Ⓐ Ⓑ Ⓒ Ⓓ	77	Ⓐ Ⓑ Ⓒ Ⓓ	97	Ⓐ Ⓑ Ⓒ Ⓓ
18	Ⓐ Ⓑ Ⓒ	38	Ⓐ Ⓑ Ⓒ	58	Ⓐ Ⓑ Ⓒ Ⓓ	78	Ⓐ Ⓑ Ⓒ Ⓓ	98	Ⓐ Ⓑ Ⓒ Ⓓ
19	Ⓐ Ⓑ Ⓒ	39	Ⓐ Ⓑ Ⓒ	59	Ⓐ Ⓑ Ⓒ Ⓓ	79	Ⓐ Ⓑ Ⓒ Ⓓ	99	Ⓐ Ⓑ Ⓒ Ⓓ
20	Ⓐ Ⓑ Ⓒ	40	Ⓐ Ⓑ Ⓒ	60	Ⓐ Ⓑ Ⓒ Ⓓ	80	Ⓐ Ⓑ Ⓒ Ⓓ	100	Ⓐ Ⓑ Ⓒ Ⓓ

READING TEST (PART 5-7)

#		#		#		#		#	
101	Ⓐ Ⓑ Ⓒ Ⓓ	121	Ⓐ Ⓑ Ⓒ Ⓓ	141	Ⓐ Ⓑ Ⓒ Ⓓ	161	Ⓐ Ⓑ Ⓒ Ⓓ	181	Ⓐ Ⓑ Ⓒ Ⓓ
102	Ⓐ Ⓑ Ⓒ Ⓓ	122	Ⓐ Ⓑ Ⓒ Ⓓ	142	Ⓐ Ⓑ Ⓒ Ⓓ	162	Ⓐ Ⓑ Ⓒ Ⓓ	182	Ⓐ Ⓑ Ⓒ Ⓓ
103	Ⓐ Ⓑ Ⓒ Ⓓ	123	Ⓐ Ⓑ Ⓒ Ⓓ	143	Ⓐ Ⓑ Ⓒ Ⓓ	163	Ⓐ Ⓑ Ⓒ Ⓓ	183	Ⓐ Ⓑ Ⓒ Ⓓ
104	Ⓐ Ⓑ Ⓒ Ⓓ	124	Ⓐ Ⓑ Ⓒ Ⓓ	144	Ⓐ Ⓑ Ⓒ Ⓓ	164	Ⓐ Ⓑ Ⓒ Ⓓ	184	Ⓐ Ⓑ Ⓒ Ⓓ
105	Ⓐ Ⓑ Ⓒ Ⓓ	125	Ⓐ Ⓑ Ⓒ Ⓓ	145	Ⓐ Ⓑ Ⓒ Ⓓ	165	Ⓐ Ⓑ Ⓒ Ⓓ	185	Ⓐ Ⓑ Ⓒ Ⓓ
106	Ⓐ Ⓑ Ⓒ Ⓓ	126	Ⓐ Ⓑ Ⓒ Ⓓ	146	Ⓐ Ⓑ Ⓒ Ⓓ	166	Ⓐ Ⓑ Ⓒ Ⓓ	186	Ⓐ Ⓑ Ⓒ Ⓓ
107	Ⓐ Ⓑ Ⓒ Ⓓ	127	Ⓐ Ⓑ Ⓒ Ⓓ	147	Ⓐ Ⓑ Ⓒ Ⓓ	167	Ⓐ Ⓑ Ⓒ Ⓓ	187	Ⓐ Ⓑ Ⓒ Ⓓ
108	Ⓐ Ⓑ Ⓒ Ⓓ	128	Ⓐ Ⓑ Ⓒ Ⓓ	148	Ⓐ Ⓑ Ⓒ Ⓓ	168	Ⓐ Ⓑ Ⓒ Ⓓ	188	Ⓐ Ⓑ Ⓒ Ⓓ
109	Ⓐ Ⓑ Ⓒ Ⓓ	129	Ⓐ Ⓑ Ⓒ Ⓓ	149	Ⓐ Ⓑ Ⓒ Ⓓ	169	Ⓐ Ⓑ Ⓒ Ⓓ	189	Ⓐ Ⓑ Ⓒ Ⓓ
110	Ⓐ Ⓑ Ⓒ Ⓓ	130	Ⓐ Ⓑ Ⓒ Ⓓ	150	Ⓐ Ⓑ Ⓒ Ⓓ	170	Ⓐ Ⓑ Ⓒ Ⓓ	190	Ⓐ Ⓑ Ⓒ Ⓓ
111	Ⓐ Ⓑ Ⓒ Ⓓ	131	Ⓐ Ⓑ Ⓒ Ⓓ	151	Ⓐ Ⓑ Ⓒ Ⓓ	171	Ⓐ Ⓑ Ⓒ Ⓓ	191	Ⓐ Ⓑ Ⓒ Ⓓ
112	Ⓐ Ⓑ Ⓒ Ⓓ	132	Ⓐ Ⓑ Ⓒ Ⓓ	152	Ⓐ Ⓑ Ⓒ Ⓓ	172	Ⓐ Ⓑ Ⓒ Ⓓ	192	Ⓐ Ⓑ Ⓒ Ⓓ
113	Ⓐ Ⓑ Ⓒ Ⓓ	133	Ⓐ Ⓑ Ⓒ Ⓓ	153	Ⓐ Ⓑ Ⓒ Ⓓ	173	Ⓐ Ⓑ Ⓒ Ⓓ	193	Ⓐ Ⓑ Ⓒ Ⓓ
114	Ⓐ Ⓑ Ⓒ Ⓓ	134	Ⓐ Ⓑ Ⓒ Ⓓ	154	Ⓐ Ⓑ Ⓒ Ⓓ	174	Ⓐ Ⓑ Ⓒ Ⓓ	194	Ⓐ Ⓑ Ⓒ Ⓓ
115	Ⓐ Ⓑ Ⓒ Ⓓ	135	Ⓐ Ⓑ Ⓒ Ⓓ	155	Ⓐ Ⓑ Ⓒ Ⓓ	175	Ⓐ Ⓑ Ⓒ Ⓓ	195	Ⓐ Ⓑ Ⓒ Ⓓ
116	Ⓐ Ⓑ Ⓒ Ⓓ	136	Ⓐ Ⓑ Ⓒ Ⓓ	156	Ⓐ Ⓑ Ⓒ Ⓓ	176	Ⓐ Ⓑ Ⓒ Ⓓ	196	Ⓐ Ⓑ Ⓒ Ⓓ
117	Ⓐ Ⓑ Ⓒ Ⓓ	137	Ⓐ Ⓑ Ⓒ Ⓓ	157	Ⓐ Ⓑ Ⓒ Ⓓ	177	Ⓐ Ⓑ Ⓒ Ⓓ	197	Ⓐ Ⓑ Ⓒ Ⓓ
118	Ⓐ Ⓑ Ⓒ Ⓓ	138	Ⓐ Ⓑ Ⓒ Ⓓ	158	Ⓐ Ⓑ Ⓒ Ⓓ	178	Ⓐ Ⓑ Ⓒ Ⓓ	198	Ⓐ Ⓑ Ⓒ Ⓓ
119	Ⓐ Ⓑ Ⓒ Ⓓ	139	Ⓐ Ⓑ Ⓒ Ⓓ	159	Ⓐ Ⓑ Ⓒ Ⓓ	179	Ⓐ Ⓑ Ⓒ Ⓓ	199	Ⓐ Ⓑ Ⓒ Ⓓ
120	Ⓐ Ⓑ Ⓒ Ⓓ	140	Ⓐ Ⓑ Ⓒ Ⓓ	160	Ⓐ Ⓑ Ⓒ Ⓓ	180	Ⓐ Ⓑ Ⓒ Ⓓ	200	Ⓐ Ⓑ Ⓒ Ⓓ

ANSWER SHEET

Admission No.

N A M E

LISTENING TEST (PART 1-4)

1 Ⓐ Ⓑ Ⓒ Ⓓ	21 Ⓐ Ⓑ Ⓒ Ⓓ	41 Ⓐ Ⓑ Ⓒ Ⓓ	61 Ⓐ Ⓑ Ⓒ Ⓓ	81 Ⓐ Ⓑ Ⓒ Ⓓ
2 Ⓐ Ⓑ Ⓒ Ⓓ	22 Ⓐ Ⓑ Ⓒ Ⓓ	42 Ⓐ Ⓑ Ⓒ Ⓓ	62 Ⓐ Ⓑ Ⓒ Ⓓ	82 Ⓐ Ⓑ Ⓒ Ⓓ
3 Ⓐ Ⓑ Ⓒ Ⓓ	23 Ⓐ Ⓑ Ⓒ Ⓓ	43 Ⓐ Ⓑ Ⓒ Ⓓ	63 Ⓐ Ⓑ Ⓒ Ⓓ	83 Ⓐ Ⓑ Ⓒ Ⓓ
4 Ⓐ Ⓑ Ⓒ Ⓓ	24 Ⓐ Ⓑ Ⓒ Ⓓ	44 Ⓐ Ⓑ Ⓒ Ⓓ	64 Ⓐ Ⓑ Ⓒ Ⓓ	84 Ⓐ Ⓑ Ⓒ Ⓓ
5 Ⓐ Ⓑ Ⓒ Ⓓ	25 Ⓐ Ⓑ Ⓒ Ⓓ	45 Ⓐ Ⓑ Ⓒ Ⓓ	65 Ⓐ Ⓑ Ⓒ Ⓓ	85 Ⓐ Ⓑ Ⓒ Ⓓ
6 Ⓐ Ⓑ Ⓒ Ⓓ	26 Ⓐ Ⓑ Ⓒ Ⓓ	46 Ⓐ Ⓑ Ⓒ Ⓓ	66 Ⓐ Ⓑ Ⓒ Ⓓ	86 Ⓐ Ⓑ Ⓒ Ⓓ
7 Ⓐ Ⓑ Ⓒ	27 Ⓐ Ⓑ Ⓒ Ⓓ	47 Ⓐ Ⓑ Ⓒ Ⓓ	67 Ⓐ Ⓑ Ⓒ Ⓓ	87 Ⓐ Ⓑ Ⓒ Ⓓ
8 Ⓐ Ⓑ Ⓒ	28 Ⓐ Ⓑ Ⓒ Ⓓ	48 Ⓐ Ⓑ Ⓒ Ⓓ	68 Ⓐ Ⓑ Ⓒ Ⓓ	88 Ⓐ Ⓑ Ⓒ Ⓓ
9 Ⓐ Ⓑ Ⓒ	29 Ⓐ Ⓑ Ⓒ Ⓓ	49 Ⓐ Ⓑ Ⓒ Ⓓ	69 Ⓐ Ⓑ Ⓒ Ⓓ	89 Ⓐ Ⓑ Ⓒ Ⓓ
10 Ⓐ Ⓑ Ⓒ	30 Ⓐ Ⓑ Ⓒ Ⓓ	50 Ⓐ Ⓑ Ⓒ Ⓓ	70 Ⓐ Ⓑ Ⓒ Ⓓ	90 Ⓐ Ⓑ Ⓒ Ⓓ
11 Ⓐ Ⓑ Ⓒ	31 Ⓐ Ⓑ Ⓒ Ⓓ	51 Ⓐ Ⓑ Ⓒ Ⓓ	71 Ⓐ Ⓑ Ⓒ Ⓓ	91 Ⓐ Ⓑ Ⓒ Ⓓ
12 Ⓐ Ⓑ Ⓒ	32 Ⓐ Ⓑ Ⓒ Ⓓ	52 Ⓐ Ⓑ Ⓒ Ⓓ	72 Ⓐ Ⓑ Ⓒ Ⓓ	92 Ⓐ Ⓑ Ⓒ Ⓓ
13 Ⓐ Ⓑ Ⓒ	33 Ⓐ Ⓑ Ⓒ Ⓓ	53 Ⓐ Ⓑ Ⓒ Ⓓ	73 Ⓐ Ⓑ Ⓒ Ⓓ	93 Ⓐ Ⓑ Ⓒ Ⓓ
14 Ⓐ Ⓑ Ⓒ	34 Ⓐ Ⓑ Ⓒ Ⓓ	54 Ⓐ Ⓑ Ⓒ Ⓓ	74 Ⓐ Ⓑ Ⓒ Ⓓ	94 Ⓐ Ⓑ Ⓒ Ⓓ
15 Ⓐ Ⓑ Ⓒ	35 Ⓐ Ⓑ Ⓒ Ⓓ	55 Ⓐ Ⓑ Ⓒ Ⓓ	75 Ⓐ Ⓑ Ⓒ Ⓓ	95 Ⓐ Ⓑ Ⓒ Ⓓ
16 Ⓐ Ⓑ Ⓒ	36 Ⓐ Ⓑ Ⓒ Ⓓ	56 Ⓐ Ⓑ Ⓒ Ⓓ	76 Ⓐ Ⓑ Ⓒ Ⓓ	96 Ⓐ Ⓑ Ⓒ Ⓓ
17 Ⓐ Ⓑ Ⓒ	37 Ⓐ Ⓑ Ⓒ Ⓓ	57 Ⓐ Ⓑ Ⓒ Ⓓ	77 Ⓐ Ⓑ Ⓒ Ⓓ	97 Ⓐ Ⓑ Ⓒ Ⓓ
18 Ⓐ Ⓑ Ⓒ	38 Ⓐ Ⓑ Ⓒ Ⓓ	58 Ⓐ Ⓑ Ⓒ Ⓓ	78 Ⓐ Ⓑ Ⓒ Ⓓ	98 Ⓐ Ⓑ Ⓒ Ⓓ
19 Ⓐ Ⓑ Ⓒ	39 Ⓐ Ⓑ Ⓒ Ⓓ	59 Ⓐ Ⓑ Ⓒ Ⓓ	79 Ⓐ Ⓑ Ⓒ Ⓓ	99 Ⓐ Ⓑ Ⓒ Ⓓ
20 Ⓐ Ⓑ Ⓒ	40 Ⓐ Ⓑ Ⓒ Ⓓ	60 Ⓐ Ⓑ Ⓒ Ⓓ	80 Ⓐ Ⓑ Ⓒ Ⓓ	100 Ⓐ Ⓑ Ⓒ Ⓓ

READING TEST (PART 5-7)

101 Ⓐ Ⓑ Ⓒ Ⓓ	121 Ⓐ Ⓑ Ⓒ Ⓓ	141 Ⓐ Ⓑ Ⓒ Ⓓ	161 Ⓐ Ⓑ Ⓒ Ⓓ	181 Ⓐ Ⓑ Ⓒ Ⓓ
102 Ⓐ Ⓑ Ⓒ Ⓓ	122 Ⓐ Ⓑ Ⓒ Ⓓ	142 Ⓐ Ⓑ Ⓒ Ⓓ	162 Ⓐ Ⓑ Ⓒ Ⓓ	182 Ⓐ Ⓑ Ⓒ Ⓓ
103 Ⓐ Ⓑ Ⓒ Ⓓ	123 Ⓐ Ⓑ Ⓒ Ⓓ	143 Ⓐ Ⓑ Ⓒ Ⓓ	163 Ⓐ Ⓑ Ⓒ Ⓓ	183 Ⓐ Ⓑ Ⓒ Ⓓ
104 Ⓐ Ⓑ Ⓒ Ⓓ	124 Ⓐ Ⓑ Ⓒ Ⓓ	144 Ⓐ Ⓑ Ⓒ Ⓓ	164 Ⓐ Ⓑ Ⓒ Ⓓ	184 Ⓐ Ⓑ Ⓒ Ⓓ
105 Ⓐ Ⓑ Ⓒ Ⓓ	125 Ⓐ Ⓑ Ⓒ Ⓓ	145 Ⓐ Ⓑ Ⓒ Ⓓ	165 Ⓐ Ⓑ Ⓒ Ⓓ	185 Ⓐ Ⓑ Ⓒ Ⓓ
106 Ⓐ Ⓑ Ⓒ Ⓓ	126 Ⓐ Ⓑ Ⓒ Ⓓ	146 Ⓐ Ⓑ Ⓒ Ⓓ	166 Ⓐ Ⓑ Ⓒ Ⓓ	186 Ⓐ Ⓑ Ⓒ Ⓓ
107 Ⓐ Ⓑ Ⓒ Ⓓ	127 Ⓐ Ⓑ Ⓒ Ⓓ	147 Ⓐ Ⓑ Ⓒ Ⓓ	167 Ⓐ Ⓑ Ⓒ Ⓓ	187 Ⓐ Ⓑ Ⓒ Ⓓ
108 Ⓐ Ⓑ Ⓒ Ⓓ	128 Ⓐ Ⓑ Ⓒ Ⓓ	148 Ⓐ Ⓑ Ⓒ Ⓓ	168 Ⓐ Ⓑ Ⓒ Ⓓ	188 Ⓐ Ⓑ Ⓒ Ⓓ
109 Ⓐ Ⓑ Ⓒ Ⓓ	129 Ⓐ Ⓑ Ⓒ Ⓓ	149 Ⓐ Ⓑ Ⓒ Ⓓ	169 Ⓐ Ⓑ Ⓒ Ⓓ	189 Ⓐ Ⓑ Ⓒ Ⓓ
110 Ⓐ Ⓑ Ⓒ Ⓓ	130 Ⓐ Ⓑ Ⓒ Ⓓ	150 Ⓐ Ⓑ Ⓒ Ⓓ	170 Ⓐ Ⓑ Ⓒ Ⓓ	190 Ⓐ Ⓑ Ⓒ Ⓓ
111 Ⓐ Ⓑ Ⓒ Ⓓ	131 Ⓐ Ⓑ Ⓒ Ⓓ	151 Ⓐ Ⓑ Ⓒ Ⓓ	171 Ⓐ Ⓑ Ⓒ Ⓓ	191 Ⓐ Ⓑ Ⓒ Ⓓ
112 Ⓐ Ⓑ Ⓒ Ⓓ	132 Ⓐ Ⓑ Ⓒ Ⓓ	152 Ⓐ Ⓑ Ⓒ Ⓓ	172 Ⓐ Ⓑ Ⓒ Ⓓ	192 Ⓐ Ⓑ Ⓒ Ⓓ
113 Ⓐ Ⓑ Ⓒ Ⓓ	133 Ⓐ Ⓑ Ⓒ Ⓓ	153 Ⓐ Ⓑ Ⓒ Ⓓ	173 Ⓐ Ⓑ Ⓒ Ⓓ	193 Ⓐ Ⓑ Ⓒ Ⓓ
114 Ⓐ Ⓑ Ⓒ Ⓓ	134 Ⓐ Ⓑ Ⓒ Ⓓ	154 Ⓐ Ⓑ Ⓒ Ⓓ	174 Ⓐ Ⓑ Ⓒ Ⓓ	194 Ⓐ Ⓑ Ⓒ Ⓓ
115 Ⓐ Ⓑ Ⓒ Ⓓ	135 Ⓐ Ⓑ Ⓒ Ⓓ	155 Ⓐ Ⓑ Ⓒ Ⓓ	175 Ⓐ Ⓑ Ⓒ Ⓓ	195 Ⓐ Ⓑ Ⓒ Ⓓ
116 Ⓐ Ⓑ Ⓒ Ⓓ	136 Ⓐ Ⓑ Ⓒ Ⓓ	156 Ⓐ Ⓑ Ⓒ Ⓓ	176 Ⓐ Ⓑ Ⓒ Ⓓ	196 Ⓐ Ⓑ Ⓒ Ⓓ
117 Ⓐ Ⓑ Ⓒ Ⓓ	137 Ⓐ Ⓑ Ⓒ Ⓓ	157 Ⓐ Ⓑ Ⓒ Ⓓ	177 Ⓐ Ⓑ Ⓒ Ⓓ	197 Ⓐ Ⓑ Ⓒ Ⓓ
118 Ⓐ Ⓑ Ⓒ Ⓓ	138 Ⓐ Ⓑ Ⓒ Ⓓ	158 Ⓐ Ⓑ Ⓒ Ⓓ	178 Ⓐ Ⓑ Ⓒ Ⓓ	198 Ⓐ Ⓑ Ⓒ Ⓓ
119 Ⓐ Ⓑ Ⓒ Ⓛ	139 Ⓐ Ⓑ Ⓒ Ⓓ	159 Ⓐ Ⓑ Ⓒ Ⓓ	179 Ⓐ Ⓑ Ⓒ Ⓓ	199 Ⓐ Ⓑ Ⓒ Ⓓ
120 Ⓐ Ⓑ Ⓒ Ⓓ	140 Ⓐ Ⓑ Ⓒ Ⓓ	160 Ⓐ Ⓑ Ⓒ Ⓓ	180 Ⓐ Ⓑ Ⓒ Ⓓ	200 Ⓐ Ⓑ Ⓒ Ⓓ

ANSWER SHEET

Admission No.

N A M E

LISTENING TEST (PART 1-4)

#						#						#						#				
1	Ⓐ	Ⓑ	Ⓒ	Ⓓ		21	Ⓐ	Ⓑ	Ⓒ			41	Ⓐ	Ⓑ	Ⓒ	Ⓓ		61	Ⓐ	Ⓑ	Ⓒ	Ⓓ		81	Ⓐ	Ⓑ	Ⓒ	Ⓓ
2	Ⓐ	Ⓑ	Ⓒ	Ⓓ		22	Ⓐ	Ⓑ	Ⓒ			42	Ⓐ	Ⓑ	Ⓒ	Ⓓ		62	Ⓐ	Ⓑ	Ⓒ	Ⓓ		82	Ⓐ	Ⓑ	Ⓒ	Ⓓ
3	Ⓐ	Ⓑ	Ⓒ	Ⓓ		23	Ⓐ	Ⓑ	Ⓒ			43	Ⓐ	Ⓑ	Ⓒ	Ⓓ		63	Ⓐ	Ⓑ	Ⓒ	Ⓓ		83	Ⓐ	Ⓑ	Ⓒ	Ⓓ
4	Ⓐ	Ⓑ	Ⓒ	Ⓓ		24	Ⓐ	Ⓑ	Ⓒ			44	Ⓐ	Ⓑ	Ⓒ	Ⓓ		64	Ⓐ	Ⓑ	Ⓒ	Ⓓ		84	Ⓐ	Ⓑ	Ⓒ	Ⓓ
5	Ⓐ	Ⓑ	Ⓒ	Ⓓ		25	Ⓐ	Ⓑ	Ⓒ			45	Ⓐ	Ⓑ	Ⓒ	Ⓓ		65	Ⓐ	Ⓑ	Ⓒ	Ⓓ		85	Ⓐ	Ⓑ	Ⓒ	Ⓓ
6	Ⓐ	Ⓑ	Ⓒ	Ⓓ		26	Ⓐ	Ⓑ	Ⓒ			46	Ⓐ	Ⓑ	Ⓒ	Ⓓ		66	Ⓐ	Ⓑ	Ⓒ	Ⓓ		86	Ⓐ	Ⓑ	Ⓒ	Ⓓ
7	Ⓐ	Ⓑ	Ⓒ	Ⓓ		27	Ⓐ	Ⓑ	Ⓒ			47	Ⓐ	Ⓑ	Ⓒ	Ⓓ		67	Ⓐ	Ⓑ	Ⓒ	Ⓓ		87	Ⓐ	Ⓑ	Ⓒ	Ⓓ
8	Ⓐ	Ⓑ	Ⓒ	Ⓓ		28	Ⓐ	Ⓑ	Ⓒ			48	Ⓐ	Ⓑ	Ⓒ	Ⓓ		68	Ⓐ	Ⓑ	Ⓒ	Ⓓ		88	Ⓐ	Ⓑ	Ⓒ	Ⓓ
9	Ⓐ	Ⓑ	Ⓒ	Ⓓ		29	Ⓐ	Ⓑ	Ⓒ			49	Ⓐ	Ⓑ	Ⓒ	Ⓓ		69	Ⓐ	Ⓑ	Ⓒ	Ⓓ		89	Ⓐ	Ⓑ	Ⓒ	Ⓓ
10	Ⓐ	Ⓑ	Ⓒ	Ⓓ		30	Ⓐ	Ⓑ	Ⓒ			50	Ⓐ	Ⓑ	Ⓒ	Ⓓ		70	Ⓐ	Ⓑ	Ⓒ	Ⓓ		90	Ⓐ	Ⓑ	Ⓒ	Ⓓ
11	Ⓐ	Ⓑ	Ⓒ	Ⓓ		31	Ⓐ	Ⓑ	Ⓒ			51	Ⓐ	Ⓑ	Ⓒ	Ⓓ		71	Ⓐ	Ⓑ	Ⓒ	Ⓓ		91	Ⓐ	Ⓑ	Ⓒ	Ⓓ
12	Ⓐ	Ⓑ	Ⓒ	Ⓓ		32	Ⓐ	Ⓑ	Ⓒ			52	Ⓐ	Ⓑ	Ⓒ	Ⓓ		72	Ⓐ	Ⓑ	Ⓒ	Ⓓ		92	Ⓐ	Ⓑ	Ⓒ	Ⓓ
13	Ⓐ	Ⓑ	Ⓒ	Ⓓ		33	Ⓐ	Ⓑ	Ⓒ			53	Ⓐ	Ⓑ	Ⓒ	Ⓓ		73	Ⓐ	Ⓑ	Ⓒ	Ⓓ		93	Ⓐ	Ⓑ	Ⓒ	Ⓓ
14	Ⓐ	Ⓑ	Ⓒ	Ⓓ		34	Ⓐ	Ⓑ	Ⓒ			54	Ⓐ	Ⓑ	Ⓒ	Ⓓ		74	Ⓐ	Ⓑ	Ⓒ	Ⓓ		94	Ⓐ	Ⓑ	Ⓒ	Ⓓ
15	Ⓐ	Ⓑ	Ⓒ	Ⓓ		35	Ⓐ	Ⓑ	Ⓒ			55	Ⓐ	Ⓑ	Ⓒ	Ⓓ		75	Ⓐ	Ⓑ	Ⓒ	Ⓓ		95	Ⓐ	Ⓑ	Ⓒ	Ⓓ
16	Ⓐ	Ⓑ	Ⓒ	Ⓓ		36	Ⓐ	Ⓑ	Ⓒ			56	Ⓐ	Ⓑ	Ⓒ	Ⓓ		76	Ⓐ	Ⓑ	Ⓒ	Ⓓ		96	Ⓐ	Ⓑ	Ⓒ	Ⓓ
17	Ⓐ	Ⓑ	Ⓒ	Ⓓ		37	Ⓐ	Ⓑ	Ⓒ			57	Ⓐ	Ⓑ	Ⓒ	Ⓓ		77	Ⓐ	Ⓑ	Ⓒ	Ⓓ		97	Ⓐ	Ⓑ	Ⓒ	Ⓓ
18	Ⓐ	Ⓑ	Ⓒ	Ⓓ		38	Ⓐ	Ⓑ	Ⓒ			58	Ⓐ	Ⓑ	Ⓒ	Ⓓ		78	Ⓐ	Ⓑ	Ⓒ	Ⓓ		98	Ⓐ	Ⓑ	Ⓒ	Ⓓ
19	Ⓐ	Ⓑ	Ⓒ	Ⓓ		39	Ⓐ	Ⓑ	Ⓒ			59	Ⓐ	Ⓑ	Ⓒ	Ⓓ		79	Ⓐ	Ⓑ	Ⓒ	Ⓓ		99	Ⓐ	Ⓑ	Ⓒ	Ⓓ
20	Ⓐ	Ⓑ	Ⓒ	Ⓓ		40	Ⓐ	Ⓑ	Ⓒ			60	Ⓐ	Ⓑ	Ⓒ	Ⓓ		80	Ⓐ	Ⓑ	Ⓒ	Ⓓ		100	Ⓐ	Ⓑ	Ⓒ	Ⓓ

READING TEST (PART 5-7)

#					#					#					#					#			
101	Ⓐ	Ⓑ	Ⓒ	Ⓓ		121	Ⓐ	Ⓑ	Ⓒ	Ⓓ		141	Ⓐ	Ⓑ	Ⓒ	Ⓓ		161	Ⓐ	Ⓑ	Ⓒ	Ⓓ		181	Ⓐ	Ⓑ	Ⓒ	Ⓓ
102	Ⓐ	Ⓑ	Ⓒ	Ⓓ		122	Ⓐ	Ⓑ	Ⓒ	Ⓓ		142	Ⓐ	Ⓑ	Ⓒ	Ⓓ		162	Ⓐ	Ⓑ	Ⓒ	Ⓓ		182	Ⓐ	Ⓑ	Ⓒ	Ⓓ
103	Ⓐ	Ⓑ	Ⓒ	Ⓓ		123	Ⓐ	Ⓑ	Ⓒ	Ⓓ		143	Ⓐ	Ⓑ	Ⓒ	Ⓓ		163	Ⓐ	Ⓑ	Ⓒ	Ⓓ		183	Ⓐ	Ⓑ	Ⓒ	Ⓓ
104	Ⓐ	Ⓑ	Ⓒ	Ⓓ		124	Ⓐ	Ⓑ	Ⓒ	Ⓓ		144	Ⓐ	Ⓑ	Ⓒ	Ⓓ		164	Ⓐ	Ⓑ	Ⓒ	Ⓓ		184	Ⓐ	Ⓑ	Ⓒ	Ⓓ
105	Ⓐ	Ⓑ	Ⓒ	Ⓓ		125	Ⓐ	Ⓑ	Ⓒ	Ⓓ		145	Ⓐ	Ⓑ	Ⓒ	Ⓓ		165	Ⓐ	Ⓑ	Ⓒ	Ⓓ		185	Ⓐ	Ⓑ	Ⓒ	Ⓓ
106	Ⓐ	Ⓑ	Ⓒ	Ⓓ		126	Ⓐ	Ⓑ	Ⓒ	Ⓓ		146	Ⓐ	Ⓑ	Ⓒ	Ⓓ		166	Ⓐ	Ⓑ	Ⓒ	Ⓓ		186	Ⓐ	Ⓑ	Ⓒ	Ⓓ
107	Ⓐ	Ⓑ	Ⓒ	Ⓓ		127	Ⓐ	Ⓑ	Ⓒ	Ⓓ		147	Ⓐ	Ⓑ	Ⓒ	Ⓓ		167	Ⓐ	Ⓑ	Ⓒ	Ⓓ		187	Ⓐ	Ⓑ	Ⓒ	Ⓓ
108	Ⓐ	Ⓑ	Ⓒ	Ⓓ		128	Ⓐ	Ⓑ	Ⓒ	Ⓓ		148	Ⓐ	Ⓑ	Ⓒ	Ⓓ		168	Ⓐ	Ⓑ	Ⓒ	Ⓓ		188	Ⓐ	Ⓑ	Ⓒ	Ⓓ
109	Ⓐ	Ⓑ	Ⓒ	Ⓓ		129	Ⓐ	Ⓑ	Ⓒ	Ⓓ		149	Ⓐ	Ⓑ	Ⓒ	Ⓓ		169	Ⓐ	Ⓑ	Ⓒ	Ⓓ		189	Ⓐ	Ⓑ	Ⓒ	Ⓓ
110	Ⓐ	Ⓑ	Ⓒ	Ⓓ		130	Ⓐ	Ⓑ	Ⓒ	Ⓓ		150	Ⓐ	Ⓑ	Ⓒ	Ⓓ		170	Ⓐ	Ⓑ	Ⓒ	Ⓓ		190	Ⓐ	Ⓑ	Ⓒ	Ⓓ
111	Ⓐ	Ⓑ	Ⓒ	Ⓓ		131	Ⓐ	Ⓑ	Ⓒ	Ⓓ		151	Ⓐ	Ⓑ	Ⓒ	Ⓓ		171	Ⓐ	Ⓑ	Ⓒ	Ⓓ		191	Ⓐ	Ⓑ	Ⓒ	Ⓓ
112	Ⓐ	Ⓑ	Ⓒ	Ⓓ		132	Ⓐ	Ⓑ	Ⓒ	Ⓓ		152	Ⓐ	Ⓑ	Ⓒ	Ⓓ		172	Ⓐ	Ⓑ	Ⓒ	Ⓓ		192	Ⓐ	Ⓑ	Ⓒ	Ⓓ
113	Ⓐ	Ⓑ	Ⓒ	Ⓓ		133	Ⓐ	Ⓑ	Ⓒ	Ⓓ		153	Ⓐ	Ⓑ	Ⓒ	Ⓓ		173	Ⓐ	Ⓑ	Ⓒ	Ⓓ		193	Ⓐ	Ⓑ	Ⓒ	Ⓓ
114	Ⓐ	Ⓑ	Ⓒ	Ⓓ		134	Ⓐ	Ⓑ	Ⓒ	Ⓓ		154	Ⓐ	Ⓑ	Ⓒ	Ⓓ		174	Ⓐ	Ⓑ	Ⓒ	Ⓓ		194	Ⓐ	Ⓑ	Ⓒ	Ⓓ
115	Ⓐ	Ⓑ	Ⓒ	Ⓓ		135	Ⓐ	Ⓑ	Ⓒ	Ⓓ		155	Ⓐ	Ⓑ	Ⓒ	Ⓓ		175	Ⓐ	Ⓑ	Ⓒ	Ⓓ		195	Ⓐ	Ⓑ	Ⓒ	Ⓓ
116	Ⓐ	Ⓑ	Ⓒ	Ⓓ		136	Ⓐ	Ⓑ	Ⓒ	Ⓓ		156	Ⓐ	Ⓑ	Ⓒ	Ⓓ		176	Ⓐ	Ⓑ	Ⓒ	Ⓓ		196	Ⓐ	Ⓑ	Ⓒ	Ⓓ
117	Ⓐ	Ⓑ	Ⓒ	Ⓓ		137	Ⓐ	Ⓑ	Ⓒ	Ⓓ		157	Ⓐ	Ⓑ	Ⓒ	Ⓓ		177	Ⓐ	Ⓑ	Ⓒ	Ⓓ		197	Ⓐ	Ⓑ	Ⓒ	Ⓓ
118	Ⓐ	Ⓑ	Ⓒ	Ⓓ		138	Ⓐ	Ⓑ	Ⓒ	Ⓓ		158	Ⓐ	Ⓑ	Ⓒ	Ⓓ		178	Ⓐ	Ⓑ	Ⓒ	Ⓓ		198	Ⓐ	Ⓑ	Ⓒ	Ⓓ
119	Ⓐ	Ⓑ	Ⓒ	Ⓓ		139	Ⓐ	Ⓑ	Ⓒ	Ⓓ		159	Ⓐ	Ⓑ	Ⓒ	Ⓓ		179	Ⓐ	Ⓑ	Ⓒ	Ⓓ		199	Ⓐ	Ⓑ	Ⓒ	Ⓓ
120	Ⓐ	Ⓑ	Ⓒ	Ⓓ		140	Ⓐ	Ⓑ	Ⓒ	Ⓓ		160	Ⓐ	Ⓑ	Ⓒ	Ⓓ		180	Ⓐ	Ⓑ	Ⓒ	Ⓓ		200	Ⓐ	Ⓑ	Ⓒ	Ⓓ